SAMAELA

Venom Of God

Megan Hernandez new life is all about eradicating drug lords and cartels. Samael was a Talmudic figure who is an accuser, seducer and destroyer.

Much like Megan's last calling, Samael is considered to be both good and evil.!

C. C. Chamberlane

Samaela

Megan Hernandez, Volume 2

C. C. Chamberlane

Published by C. C. Chamberlane, 2022.

SAMAELA

First edition. February 16, 2022.

Copyright © 2022 C. C. Chamberlane.

ISBN: 978-1775373216

Written by C. C. Chamberlane.

Also by C. C. Chamberlane

Megan Hernandez
Samaela
The First Female Navy SEAL
Saving Ukraine

Standalone
Abbadon

SAMAELA

C. C. CHAMBERLANE

Her past life and misdeeds behind her Megan Hernandez is now fighting for a greater cause. Her friend's wife had been killed by drug lords and she would be the avenger of that death. She had fought evil a good deal of her life and had served her country with honor and distinction. It was all top-secret, but she knew she had done what her country required of her.

She would now help in her own way, fighting the local evils that threatened the American way of life.

If you have comments or ideas, please email us directly at CCChamberlane@gmail.com

@ccchamberlane

SAMAELA

ISBN Print – 978-1-7753732-1-6
Copyright 2018 C. C. CHAMBERLANE
Published by C. C. Chamberlane

Thank you for respecting the hard work of this author.

Acknowledgements

After a rousing response to ABBADON, C.C.Chamberlane's first book, I am pleased to offer the follow up novel for your reading pleasure. This book is dedicated to all the loyal fans who have read Abbadon, and I hope you like this one even more. Thank you all for your support.

About the Author – C.C. Chamberlane

This is the second fact-influenced-fiction crime novel in a series that will feature the exploits of Megan Hernandez. I really hope you enjoy this second novel in the series. Follow her as she continues to make the world a better place, according to her own unique set of rules.

I have always been a true crime type person as these stories are multi-layered and stimulate deep thought. I find both the character development and plot development fascinating and have always been a fan.

Keep an eye on our Facebook page at C.C.Chamberlane and watch for the next title in the series.

Prologue

Megan Hernandez, or Meg as her friends always called her, was destined for something in the military or law enforcement from the day she was born. Her father and grandfather were both skilled military men and her mother was a decorated detective. She was always fascinated by the stories each person would tell about their exploits, challenges, and accomplishments. As she grew older, the stories and lessons learned around the dinner table helped shape who she would become.

Meg was also easy on the eyes, benefitting from the genes provided by a Mexican father and white mother. She was above average height for a woman and heavier too. Of course, that extra weight was pure, battle-honed muscle. She was no model. She was a government trained killing machine who had tremendous success in the military and elsewhere.

Meg was never encumbered by any thoughts about girls being "weaker" or less important than boys. The concept was completely foreign to everyone she knew and grew up with. Her whole family ensured that she knew equality, even superiority, was built into her DNA. As such, she excelled in all aspects of her training once she entered the military. Megan was frequently recognized as top of class.

She was never sure why she went the direction she did, but Megan knew she was making a real difference once she finally found her true calling. This calling was what came after her discharge.

Her new "career" really was thrust upon her by accident.

She started dating a fellow a couple of years after her release from the special forces, and things were good at first. They took a turn down a bad path early in the relationship however and, being who she was, Meg was not about to put up with any crap. Bobby had begun to abuse her emotionally and even physically. Meg wasn't going to report him or go to the police, She would handle the problem herself, as she always had. She had handled so many problems for so many other people she gave only the briefest of thought to why she would not do so for herself.

She knew she couldn't simply shoot her abusive boyfriend. Well, she was certainly capable of it, but she would need to be incredibly careful. She considered poison, cutting the brake lines, tons of ideas went through her head. She was a trained killer however, and she knew that any of those methods would likely land her in prison. There were much better ways to get rid of someone and she knew many of them.

Of course, the spouse/partner was always the first place the police looked, and poison was a frequent weapon of choice in those cases. Especially when women killed. They seemed to like the detachment and distance that using poison provided. There are also many poisons that could be "accidentally" ingested. Megan knew that when women were involved poison was a real favorite, except for Meg, her favorite was still the garotte.

There were so many poisons that occur naturally and can be easily disguised and given to someone. Aconite , or Wolfsbane, is one of those. Even touching the leaves of the plant can be lethal, causing arrhythmic heart function that leads to the victim suffocating. Others like Belladonna and Hemlock are more well known and equally effective.

While poison was easy and clean it simply was not an option. If they found out she was, or had been dating Bobby, using poison would put her squarely in the spotlight of the investigation. She was known to have dated him and would certainly be a suspect. This had to be a very well thought-out and comprehensive plan. Megan set about designing such a plan and then putting it into action. She finished him off without fanfare or drawing attention to herself and that was that. She was free to move on.

Now that her ex-boyfriend was out of the picture, Meg decided to take a year off. She was concerned for herself and believed time away would be the solution.

She didn't really like who she had become and set out to get back to who she thought she was. Get back to who she was when she was on the teams.

Now that she had eliminated Bobby and a few other miscreants, it was time for a rest. She genuinely wanted to be just another California surf-bum, although some days it seemed like trouble just followed her around.

Chapter One – Background

Since I was last active, I have given a great deal of thought to my chosen path. I was feeling guilty over what I had done and even how I had done it. Guilt was not something I had ever experienced before. The government trained me to do a job and I did that job, end of story. But it was never really the end of the story. I frequently found myself out of sorts, sometimes confused and other times simply angry. I knew I had to do something.

I finally sought some help through the VA and found a psychologist I believe helps me. She certainly does not know the whole story, nor do I plan to share what I have been doing since my release with her, or anyone else for that matter. She does know snippets of my past from my active service days though. I had to have a way to explain my feelings.

When we are together, we speak more about general feelings, and I sprinkle in a little about some of what happened when I was operating. I have not divulged the depth of the torture I endured nor the jumbled thoughts I have about my past. I just don't see what would be gained by revealing too much. I do enjoy our sessions however, and I will likely continue with them. She provides me a relatively safe haven to discuss things I am unable to share with anyone else. I remain guarded in my comments but that is more about self-preservation than psychology.

I have thought long and hard about Bobby and the other scumbags I eradicated during the last phase of my post-special forces' life. I certainly don't lose any sleep when I think about any of them. At least I try not to lose sleep. They earned the ends they met, each one of them. These were bad men who were not likely going to be stopped via legal means.

The law had tried and failed with most of these wastes of skin, so someone had to take the reins. I do remain somewhat concerned about how easily I slipped into inflicting pain and punishment on my victims, however. I understood why I would "enjoy" doing that to Bobby, because it was so intimately personal for me, but that didn't help explain the others.

I kept telling myself they deserved it but when I flashed back to my own torture I was conflicted. How could ANY human being deserve to be treated in that way? I decided that no matter what I did next or how I was directed in my life that I would never resort to torture again. Unless, of course, it was absolutely necessary.

I knew the effects of torture and I was well aware of how to extract truth. My training provided me with all the tools I needed to get the information I required out of just about anyone. I had been taught it was typically more psychology than brute force anyway.

I had extensive training in both areas, I just had to keep that training top of mind and not let anger take over again.

What was previously known as typical torture very seldom yielded factual and actionable intelligence anyway. Often it was simply the captor finally agreeing with whatever was being presented in hopes of making the pain stop.

In many cases, once the "confession" was extracted the pain stopped in the most final of ways. This usually only happened after the confession was used to discredit the captor's country of origin or the group for which he was fighting.

My thoughts soon drifted back to the more conventional. Over the last year I had not really communicated much with Norie but had maintained my friendships and social life. I continue to hang with Kathy, Jonathon, Angela, and Luke. I attend most of their gatherings and I still work out with the girls regularly, in addition to my other training. It was, at this point, a somewhat normal and enjoyable life. The life I thought I wanted.

We also all stay connected with Colin Sharpe.

He is still a Special Agent and despite his failure to find that nasty serial killer that was taking out woman-beaters he was finally promoted. He seems the same to us and when we are at parties, he continues to play it close to the vest. On the good side, he appears to have almost recovered from his wife's demise.

Recently, he even brought a date to one of the gatherings. It didn't appear to be anything serious but, oddly, I found myself feeling a little jealous. I had feelings for people who were friends before, but it had never worked out that well. I tried to simply be happy for him, as any friend would. Muddying my waters with a relationship just did not seem like a great idea.

Everyone responds to losses like he experienced in unique ways. Colin was no different than any other human being in that regard.

Most go through the seven stages of grief, but all move at a different pace. Some lagging at one level more than others. It is typical of the human condition. It is something we all experience at various times in our lives due to circumstances and everyone processes the situations in unique ways.

To all outward appearances though, Colin seemed to have recovered. He appeared to be at the acceptance level. That was when you were finally at a point where you understood your loss, you had grieved appropriately, and arrived at what people like to call closure.

I always thought closure was more of a unicorn than a truth. People liked to think it happened, but I did not believe these life events ever were completely closed. For Colin I thought, knowing him as I did, that he would soon enter an eighth level of grief, revenge. There is a lot of talk about revenge. They say it tears you up and all that stuff. I wasn't too sure about that either. I had tasted revenge and it was certainly not the worst dish I had ever experienced, cold or hot.

He might not refer to it as revenge or even consciously be aware of it, but I was sure that stage would drive his life for the foreseeable future. I knew this more than most and I got that vibe from Colin every now and then.

Chapter Two – Reconnecting with Norie

I had not seen Norie in a little more than a year. We spoke on the telephone every now and then, so we kept up with current happenings. I watched her blossom in her new position. I was pleased to hear that Norie had been doing very well as an Assistant District Attorney for Los Angeles county. In fact, she was pretty much top of the heap in that office. She was extremely intelligent and, thanks to her work as a defense attorney, had a deep understanding of defense strategies. That made her a killer ADA. She normally knew what the other side was thinking and often knew their game plan, even before it had been decided.

Usually, a lawyer would go the other way. They would toil in the District Attorney's office for a fraction of what they are worth to gain experience. Then they leave, within a few years, for the mountains of cash to be made being a defense attorney. Sleep comes less easily for criminal defense lawyers however and Norie knows that more than most. I figured the work we had done was what pushed her back onto the right side of the law.

After all, the type of thing I did was not for everyone. I should say, the type of thing WE did wasn't for everyone. I was still surprised at what Norie was able to do during our time "working" together. I am a good judge of character and simply did not think she had it in her to do the things we did.

As an Assistant District Attorney in Los Angeles Norie worked directly for Jackie Lacey. Norie respected, and perhaps even idolized, her boss Jackie Lacey. Norie was even contemplating a run at D.A. at some point because of what she saw her boss accomplish. She spoke to Jackie about it and said she would only run if Jackie was retiring though.

When Jackie said her work was not yet done and she had no intention of retiring, I think Norie felt a little relieved. She knew she could do the job, but she wanted to work more with Jackie first. She would have more time to learn and grow under Lacey's tutelage.

Jackie Lacey is the current District Attorney for Los Angeles. She was top of her class at U.C Irvine and again at USC's Gould School of Law. When she ran for the DA's office in 2012, she was virtually a lock on being elected. Her credentials and resume are second-to-none and she is a captivating public speaker. Although she never played the race or gender cards, she knew that, in this day and age, both would act in her favor. She was well-aware she would have to say nothing about either and that would also benefit her in the long run. Often, allowing people to simply think what they want without prompting or selling is the best approach.

She is not only the first African American to serve as the LA District Attorney, but she is also the first woman to do so since the office was created in 1850!

At 61 years of age, she appears to be in her prime, applying her wealth of knowledge and experience to her job. She is so intelligent that she simply sees things that others cannot, situations others do not understand.

Her comprehension is amazing, and her commitment is off the charts.

Recently, she has come under fire for her reluctance to prosecute police officers when they are involved in questionable shootings. Certainly, with media coverage, cell phone videos, body cameras, and other ways for these situations to go public it is an extremely challenging time for law enforcement.

Through the narrow lens of a camera, with little surrounding context, almost any situation can look bad. It is all about perspective and timing it would seem.

Jackie Lacey is not someone who bows to public opinion though or pressure from any identifiable group. She appears to be truly agnostic whether the issue involves women, white people, black people, Hispanics, or any other identifiable group. As noted, she has not yet chosen to prosecute a police officer during her tenure. Even though there have been cases that perhaps should have gone to trial.

The most notorious one likely being the shooting of Brendon Glenn who lived near the boardwalk at Venice Beach. He seemed harmless, spending most days skateboarding up and down the beachfront. Everything changed for him in the most final of ways when the wrong police officer stopped him. Los Angeles is a very dangerous place, and I would think almost any LAPD officer could have a short fuse. The line between life and death for them is amazingly thin.

This shooting was captured on video and the city eventually paid out $4 million to Glenn's family in a wrongful death suit.

The Los Angeles Chief of Police at the time, Charlie Beck, even called publicly for his own police officer to be prosecuted. It never happened though.

Insiders claim Lacey knew she would not win at trial, even though Glenn was the third unarmed black man to be killed during her tenure. Much like a coach being extra hard on their own kids perhaps Lacey, who was raised in the South during the Jim Crow era, was doing the same thing.

She was being extra hard on her own race, regardless of the fallout from that group or any other. I am certain it was a difficult balancing act for her, but she seemed quite skilled in that area. She was able to compartmentalize her thoughts and feelings very well.

However, each of those cases would have been extremely difficult to win and she knew that. As the DA for Los Angeles, she is ultimately the one who decides whether to bring charges against someone. In many of these cases she realized that millions would be spent at trial with little confidence of success. You just never knew with a jury trial and if you lost, double jeopardy was attached. That means even if evidence surfaced later, they could not re-try the case. There are precious few do-overs when it comes to the law.

Also, a tenuous relationship with law enforcement would be further strained and ultimately the officer would go free. All that would happen would be heightened tensions and an even deeper distrust of the police by those whom they are charged with protecting.

There may even be riots if another police officer were tried and won his innocence. Jackie Lacey struggled with these decisions often.

The average person has such little comprehension of these circumstances it can be easy to get all riled up. It is politically correct for people to claim police brutality or excessive force, but those people have never been in that situation. An aggressive person or group, many times threatening your own life, as you try to keep the peace or enforce the law is difficult to handle.

Police officers are all trained the same way. You do your best to avoid having to fire your sidearm, it is a tool of last resort.

That was why Tasers became popular, it gave an officer another tool without resorting to deadly force.

You use all your other skills to try to de-escalate a dangerous situation. But, when push comes to shove, you are authorized to use deadly force to protect yourself or others. It is never like it is portrayed in the movies, a single well-placed shot to disable an attacker. Even at close range, a pistol is not as accurate as all those TV shows would have you believe. You never witnessed an officer shoot someone holding a hostage against them in the head. That was a job for the sniper.

You are taught to pull the trigger three times in rapid succession, aimed at the largest mass of the body, to remove the threat.

I am certainly not saying that the death of people like Brendon Glenn is in any way justified. The world would be a much better place if, when a threat was made, you could just press the pause button. A pause would give you time to fully evaluate all the possibilities. You could take the time to assess the whole situation and then safely restrain the person.

Life simply does not work that way. In law enforcement, decisions must be made in split seconds.

The bottom line is that the best decision is not always made and even though it is natural for people to want consequences, it does not always happen that way.

Those are all Jackie's worries not Norie's. While Jackie Lacey is focusing on the macro-issues of her position, she has come to rely more on Norie Mueller to handle the top cases.

Norie has been involved in many kinds of trials, from the sex abuse scandals in the entertainment industry all the way to prosecuting complex drug cases. It is these drug cases where Norie really shines. Norie's analytical mind is the main reason that Jackie has been her mentor almost since she hired Norie. They think in similar ways, and both can shut out the commentary and pressure directed at them and focus solely on the facts.

These are frequently extremely challenging and dangerous cases. The defence lawyers, oftentimes hired and paid for by a drug cartel, are very skilled at getting these people freed. Even so, Norie has had success putting away some dangerous dudes peddling drugs to our children and preying on the weakest of society.

At trial, she focuses on the effects these people are having on individuals and families. Norie uses logic and ugly facts to tug on the heart strings of even the most conservative of juries. They see the results of the poison these people are putting onto our streets and many times they end up convicting. She makes it so they simply cannot ignore the collateral damage. Norie really is a rising star who has a very bright future.

If I were ever on trial, I would not like to see her across the courtroom! I would want her on my side. That sentiment applies if I were to find myself in a brawl too.

Even amid all her success, she still wrestled with her own demons when she saw people set free who she knew were guilty. During our conversations, I could tell she hated feeling that powerless. I suppose nobody enjoys that feeling, but it really hits her hard. She knew she had done her best and should have won the case, but slick defense lawyers make a lot of money for good reason. She knew from personal experience, and success.

The people hiring them have a lot of money to pay. Sadly, in our legal system, cash really does buy the best defense. It was the dealers and their bosses who had more cash than anyone it seemed. I admired Norie for doing what she was doing and thought she was very brave. I missed hanging with her.

There was a party coming up at Kathy and Jonathon's this weekend and I decided I would call Norie and invite her as my guest. There were no men in the picture currently for me and I certainly felt no pressure to bring anyone. I never did feel that pressure, I was always good all on my own. I thought it would be a great time to reconnect with her and re-introduce her to everyone else. Things had been rather good for everyone in my circle of friends, and I wanted to expand it a little.

Jonathon and Luke's business was still rolling along and even doing better now that there were different economic pressures on people. It seemed even more important to have guys like this helping you invest these days. I had even set up an account myself, at Jonathon's insistence. He was relentless in his desire to help, and I finally capitulated.

It all started with a tech start up he knew of that really was a no-miss. It wasn't going to be as wildly successful as google or Apple, but it was still going to go big. Of course, he was accurate as usual. That first stock became the foundation of my portfolio. He turned my small $20,000 investment into $400,000 within two years! I then diversified my holdings and, with Jonathon's guidance, now had an account that topped TWO-MILLION-DOLLARS.

It still amazes me, and it seems like the more you make, the more you make! It is especially easy when you are playing with "house money" like when you're gambling. I am confident he has many clients who have done equally well thanks to him and Luke.

I invited Norie over to my place on the way to the party to stop in for a drink. When Saturday rolled around, I was stoked for another one of their beach bashes. I was anxious about seeing Norie again too. It was another glorious Southern California day, and I was looking forward to catching some waves and just hanging out. I was working in my yard when I heard the bell ring, so I just went around the side of the house.

Norie spotted me as I came around the corner and she ran to give me a huge hug. I stepped back and said how great she looked and mentioned that being a top ADA looked like it agreed with her. She always looked so well put together anyway. She was one of those people who just knew how to dress for anything.

She was wearing a sporty tank top with a loose shirt over top along with a shorter athletic skort. She was completely coordinated right down to her bright orange saucony trainers. She looked like she was about to shoot a commercial. I suppose being in the public eye the way she was you were always "on." In her position she never knew when or where a reporter would approach her. In Los Angeles there was no privacy.

It has always been that way. Like almost every other situation she found herself presented with, she was ready.

I always felt a little less womanly around Norie. I decided I would need to select a different outfit before we left for the party. We walked inside so I could fix us each a drink and the chatter didn't stop. As I mixed us a couple of dark & stormies, I was telling Norie how I had been watching her career and how happy I was for her. I said I was amazed how she could stand up to these killers and drug lords. She deflected the compliments claiming she wasn't winning enough for her likes. There were still bad guys getting away and she hated that part of her job. For Norie, every loss was personal. She felt like she had let her boss, the victims, the whole state, down when she did not win.

She asked what I had been doing to keep occupied. I said there was really no difference since before our last venture. I was still training all the time but doing a lot more surfing. In fact, I had been working with a surfing coach who was helping me get to the next level. Norie asked if he was good-looking, and I pointed out he was.

I quickly added that I had no interest in an airhead who was way too young for me anyway.

He wasn't really an airhead, and I had no idea why I felt it necessary to add that to the description. He seemed like a good kid, and he was fun to be around.

My teacher, Duke Koehner was literally born to surf. He was Gidget's real-life son and was named after Duke Kahanamoku, the father of modern-day surfing. Dukey, as he was often called, even resembled the Big Kahuna himself sometimes.

Duke Kahanamoku was of Hawaiian descent. Dukey was a mix of white, black, and Hispanic but when the sun hit him the right way while riding a wave one could almost see the Big Kahuna. He even typically surfed a long board, just like Duke. He looked so majestic standing tall on his board with the sun behind him illuminating him like a statue. He looked like he had been carved from a huge chunk of bronze with the multihued sky as his backdrop.

The original Duke won five Olympic gold medals in swimming. He was just raw, sinewy muscle with amazing core strength. He competed at Olympics in Stockholm, Antwerp and Paris and won at each. He even saved the lives of fishermen on a sinking boat once and singlehandedly started the surfing craze in Australia.

Duke lived an amazing life. If you ever want to read a remarkable story you should read about Duke Kahanamoku. Even if you have never surfed, you would still love his story.

My Duke was a little less of a big deal to be sure. He was certainly your typical California surfer-dude though. He kept his hair a little longer than the Big Kahuna but was in similar shape. Darker skin and rippling muscles with amazing core strength allowed him to do whatever he wished while on a surfboard. I marvelled at the control he had over his board and his body as if they were one. He really was turning me into a better surfer. He understood waves and boards like no other, and he was able to communicate that to students.

I had come a long way under his tutelage. I now had amazing confidence on my board and loved the feel of surfing more than ever. He even wanted me to enter a competition at Huntington Beach, aka Surf City, but I didn't really have any desire to compete for once.

I wanted to be the best surfer I could be for the sole purpose of enjoying every wave to its maximum potential. I knew Dukey was a little frustrated by this but by now we had become friends and he respected my decision.

We surfed together at least three times a week and my progress amazed me. Clearly, I knew I could never get to his level, but it was still fun to try. I just couldn't get enough of surfing. I felt like a kid riding a blue wave of power. You were always twisting, turning, and trying to read where the wave was going, anticipating subtle changes that would affect the ride.

Each wave unique, each ride a unique adventure all on its own. It really gave me immense pleasure and helped reduce tension in my life. THIS was the best kind of therapy, way better than sitting in a chair or laying on a sofa talking!

After we hashed through the details of surfing and Dukey, Norie and I sat on the patio for quite a while. After a second drink we decided we should head over to the party. After all, we didn't want to miss whatever new appetizer Jonathon was going to serve! He was the best and if I were to ever get married, I think I would want a clone of him.

We finished our drinks, jumped into my car, and headed over to Kathy's.

Chapter Three – Yet Another Fun Bash

Norie and I knocked on the front door and as Kathy opened it, we could tell the party was already in full swing. Kathy said it was great to see Norie again, we all hugged and went through the house and out to the patio. As we stepped out a bunch of people gravitated toward us including Jon, Luke, Angie, and Colin Sharpe. We said how great it was to get together again and we all had margaritas in our hands in seconds.

Jonathon had bought a system that looked like a three-part Slurpee machine. There was a large section that contained ice and crushed ice, a second section with a lime juice and sugar mixture and a third with a blend of tequila and triple sec. The thing was huge, and he drug us over to it to explain how it worked. He said he had designed it, but it was built by a local company that makes all kinds of food equipment.

It kind of resembled those giant espresso machines you see at expensive Italian restaurants. It was all gleaming stainless steel and glass, and he was clearly proud of his invention. The lime juice was even fresh as you just loaded the hopper with fresh limes, and it cut and squeezed them as required. I will say, they were some of the tastiest margaritas I had ever had! It seemed to be all everyone was drinking so I figured this would be a full Mexican theme. It wasn't Cinco de Mayo or anything, but it certainly could have been.

Norie and I went in, changed into our bathing suits and returned to the patio. Everyone was wearing either a bathing suit or board shorts as it was another perfect day at the beach. To be honest, I was itching for a little surfing so didn't want to have another drink until I did some. We were all sitting around the larger table catching up when Colin took my arm and suggested a few rides. I excused myself, we grabbed a couple of boards and paddled out.

As can happen in the ocean, there was quite a lull in waves, so we chatted idly while we drifted on our boards. We were just catching up and yakking and he said he was really glad to see me again. I echoed the sentiment and asked him how he was doing. He said work was going very well. He was a little disheartened by the fact his promotion reduced his fieldwork, but he was adapting.

He mentioned he had been working a lot of drug cases and he discovered some facts about Patti's death that were never revealed. He looked behind him and said there was a set coming and maybe we can talk about it over lunch some other day. Right now, he just wanted to surf.

I said sure, that would be great as he caught the first wave and took off. I grabbed the third and worked it hard right to the beach.

I was having a fun time and didn't want this ride to finish. Tougher to get back out to the waves but I wasn't concerned. I turned out as late as I could after an excellent ride.

I picked up my board, ran through the first few breaks and then hopped on and started paddling. As I got back next to Colin he looked over and said it looked like I had been practicing. At first, I laughed and said it was only one wave. But then I came clean and told him about Dukey and how good he was and what a great teacher he was.

He smiled over at me and said he might like to get in on some of that. I told him I would mention it to Duke and then we got back to some serious surfing. The waves were excellent, a little larger than usual, so we had to watch the undertow and where the waves were breaking.

Often, when they get larger in this area, they tend to break hard in suddenly shallow water. You really needed to pay attention to where you were because if you got too far past the break riding the wave you could get driven hard into the sand, or worse, the rocks.

It wasn't more than two waves later when my thoughts seemed prophetic. I caught a large wave and then watched as Colin flew past me.

I turned out early and as I popped back up, I saw him take a vary hard fall. His leash was still on, and I waited about twenty seconds, watching his board closely. When he still didn't pop out of the water, I paddled hard to where his board was.

I grabbed the leash and followed it to find Colin under the surf and I could see blood on his head. I grabbed an arm and pulled him up onto my back in a fireman's carry and started running to shore yelling. I set him down softly as I hit the sand. People were already waiting for me.

He was out cold it seemed, and I couldn't sense breathing, so we started CPR right away. Soon, he coughed up a small amount of water and was breathing on his own. I knew that was a good sign but then I saw the cut on his head. I first thought he had a bloody nose, but he had obviously hit a rock. It was an odd location as the cut was on the back of his head. He had evidently tumbled when the wave broke. When he spun in the water, like he was in a washing machine, was likely when he hit the rock. I've been on that wild ride more than once and they are never fun.

I wanted to call 9-1-1 but Colin was coming around and telling us it was just a surface wound. He even joked about his head damaging the rock. I looked at his eyes and examined him closely but didn't see any evidence of a concussion.

He asked how long he had been out, and someone said only a minute or two. He smiled up at me and asked if I had to give him mouth to mouth.

I looked at him, laughed and told him he couldn't possibly think I would put my lips on his mouth, did he? He recalled the comment I had made when we were surfing, more than a year ago, asking if I was going to have to save his sorry ass or not. When he did that, I figured he was okay. We would still need to keep an eye on him but there was no sense in calling 9-1-1 it seemed.

He sat up and we all walked back up to the patio, surfing finished for the day. Turned out the wound was indeed more of a surface cut after all, and the bleeding stopped on its own. I looked at him and pointed out he was right; he did have a hard melon.

He knocked on his own head, making a wooden sound and said, "I told ya, nothing to get hurt here."

We all just relaxed and enjoyed the rest of the party. Norie came over to join us and Colin was saying how much he admired her work. The two of them were like a mutual admiration society in no time. Each talking about the other in reverent tones.

Colin saying how he had seen her in court and how impressed he was. Norie adding that without the solid detective work from people like Colin her job would be so much harder. Blah, blah, blah, I excused myself to grab a fresh margarita. I loved they were getting along and catching up, but I was bored.

I went back about ten minutes later and the two of them were still on the same topic. I sat down and asked Norie about her last drug case and how it ended. She told us that before she convicted this dolt, she got him to flip on the next guy up the food chain. All she knew was it was a guy named Arturo who lived in La Jolla. Colin laughed casually and said that a drug dealer named Arturo in La Jolla should stand out like a sore thumb. Norie just smiled and told him to let her know when he found the guy.

Other than more margaritas and great cooking from Jonathon the party ended uneventfully. Before I left, Colin grabbed me and said he was serious about lunch and told me to pick a day next week.

I asked if he wanted to head up to Duke's in Malibu? I told him I hadn't seen Gidget in quite a while, and I needed a happiness fix. He agreed that was a great idea, so we decided to meet there on Wednesday. We went our separate ways, I got Norie, and we took off in an Uber.

Norie just stayed at my place, and we sat up drinking wine and talking for a good part of the night. She was saying that she loved her job, and her boss was amazing, but she still struggled with bad guys getting away. These people weren't simple bad guys though. They were powerful and wealthy drug lords much like the crime bosses back in the Mafia days. The main difference was these guys seemed to have no code of honor the way the Al Capone's of the world did. Capone did everything to try and stop the wars and get people working together. It never did really happen, but it was an innovative idea, for a criminal.

In the drug cartel world, to achieve their ends and grow their empires nobody was safe. Women, children, clergy, dogs...it simply didn't matter who was harmed or killed in their singular pursuit of wealth and power. They had no honor and certainly no compassion. They liked to use a messy and painful death in front of others to keep everyone in line. Leading by fear was their stock-in-trade.

Norie continued talking about many cases and how, even when you cut the head off the serpent, other heads would simply take over.

She had volumes of information and stated fact after fact about these groups of which I had no knowledge.

I had spent some time on an op or two in Mexico but some of these things Norie shared were new to me.

Since December 2006, when the Mexican government declared its war on organized crime, over 200,000 people had been killed. Previously, the drug cartels seemed to do as they pleased, not only under the nose of the law but seemingly, with their support. One of the most famous and lucrative of these cartels was the Sinaloa cartel, led by Joaquin Archivaldo Guzman Loera, commonly known as El Chapo.

As mean as "El Chapo" sounds it translates to "shorty" in English. I found that humorous for some reason. El Chapo's current net worth is estimated to be in the range of more than four billion US dollars! His recent capture created a split in that cartel with one side being run by his two sons, Ivan, and Jesus. The other side is run by former associates, Damaso Nunez, and his own son Damaso Serrano. This split made room for growth in other cartels operating in Mexico and the US. They were all opportunists, and this was a great one staring them all right in the face.

Of all the upstarts, Jalisco New Generation is likely the strongest competitor to Sinaloa. They own Tijuana and the important port of Manzanillo. Their complete lack of respect for law enforcement is evidenced by the army chopper they shot down in 2015 with an RPG.

To take out an armed army helo with a rocket propelled grenade is no small feat, but they did it.

Not only did they do it, but they also then bragged about it. I was surprised a team, or an operator like me, had not been sent in to destroy them. My thoughts turned quickly to how I would handle the situation back when I was still in the employ of our government.

Their current head is Ruben Oseguera, known as El Mencho. If he had a resume, it would show that he had a wide variety of jobs prior to becoming a drug lord and organized crime boss. These many jobs included avocado vendor and even police officer. In Mexico, being a police officer seemed to be great training for working in the drug trade. They often had all the connections and once they switched sides they could leverage those connections, or simply eliminate the ones who would not be helpful.

There are many other cartels operating in different geographic regions including the Knights Templar and La Familia. I couldn't help but think how these guys were great at making up gang names and assigning nicknames to their leaders. The more I heard the more ridiculous it seemed.

The Mexican government's primary target right now is Ismael "El Mayo" Zambada. He is now 69 years of age and seemingly getting ready to pass the torch, but he remains public enemy number one. This is the case for a few reasons.

With the focus on drug wars, many cartels are diversifying into multiple revenue streams. Kidnapping, extortion, human trafficking and even stealing oil are all methods for them to increase their wealth. These new areas of interest are the main reason that Mexican officials are responding to public outcry. It is not only drug users being affected any longer. It is everyone and public pressure, even in a place like Mexico, can be a powerful force.

When nobody is safe, corruption can sometimes take a back seat to fighting crime. That appears to be the scenario right now with many Mexican law enforcement and government officials willing to work with other agencies. One could say the relationship with US law enforcement has never been better, although it is kept well-hidden. I'm certain the current POTUS would not be happy if he were made aware of this level of cooperation. He clearly is not that big a fan of Mexico, or us Hispanic types.

Norie said we would have to discuss this further in the future but right now she needed some sleep. Her brain needed a rest, so I showed her to the guest room and then flopped down onto my own bed. I was asleep in minutes and slept well.

We got up at a reasonable hour and headed over to IHOP for breakfast. That place has a bit of a bad rap, but I loved the one close to my house. They made the best waffles, and I really liked all their toppings and sauces.

It was one of my few vices. We didn't talk much about anything of consequence. We just ate our breakfast and then Norie left in her car while I strolled back home, my IHOP desire sated for now.

I found myself looking ahead to Wednesday and feeling excited to see Colin. It may be a little too soon, but I was interested in seeing what might happen between the two of us. I found myself thinking maybe this friend conversion might work out this time.

I knew I would have to be patient. I certainly would not want to try to rush something like this. I was also concerned about what the others might think.

Chapter Four – Colin's Real Story

Wednesday rolled around and I took my time getting ready. I selected clothes in which I would be comfortable but perhaps showed off the fact I was a woman more than my usual attire did. This was just two friends having lunch, but I was feeling like it was going to be our first date. I wondered what Colin was thinking. Was he having the same thoughts about me?

I got into my truck and headed up to Malibu. I chose Wednesday because I knew that was one of the days that Gidget would be there. I hadn't seen her since I started taking lessons with her son Duke. I pulled into the parking lot right at noon. I walked in the front door and spotted Colin at a table, and I did my best "I'm good-looking walk" over to him.

Colin stood up and gave me a big hug and said how great it was to see me again. I couldn't help but think he was looking at this like a date too. I had only seen him a few days prior and that was a big hug. I know I was attracted to him, but it was almost a year and a half since that time. As he hugged me close, I noticed his strength and remembered carrying him out of the water. We sat down and ordered drinks.

When they arrived, he immediately raised his glass and said, "here's to the woman who saved my life." I said that may be a little too much credit, I only pulled his sorry butt out of the water. We clinked glasses, smiled at one another and he said he would return the favor any time. I laughed and said I was sure he wouldn't have to, but it was always good to have some insurance.

Just after that, Gidget dropped over to our table saying how good it was to see us again. I smiled at her and said I had a great new surfing coach. This wonderful kid named Duke. She smiled broadly and said she thought I might be the hot surfer that Dukey had told her about. I looked up at her and said, "hot surfer, huh?" We both laughed at that. I'm almost old enough to be his mother you know.

He had shared with her that his student was both pretty and an absolute bundle of muscle. I looked up and said, oh really. He didn't say that did he? She told me he had a bit of a crush on me but knew that nothing would ever come of it, so he was good just being friends. That was a bit of a relief. As I said, I really wasn't interested in getting involved with a guy like him.

Gidget hung out for a bit, and we talked about waves on various beaches and other surf stuff. She said I should really enter the US Open, Duke told her that I was easily good enough now. I explained that I did not want to turn surfing into a competition.

I then smiled and said there was no way I wanted to compete in a "seniors" division either, even though that division is only over age 35. There was NO way I was going to do anything where I was classed as a senior. She chuckled and took off to go greet another table, giving me a hug before she left.

We enjoyed a long, leisurely lunch and over dessert Colin finally shared his secret. He told me was now convinced Patti's death was murder, although it would be impossible to prove. They had set up a massive back story that made her look like a drug user. Colin never did really believe that, so he kept digging and digging. He trusted no one, well-aware that the drug cartels had deep reach into all kinds of places, even the FBI.

Colin never believed the story they created, and he knew he would have to dig further on his own. Under the guise of saying good-bye to his wife, he had managed to grab a skin sample and other DNA. He then took those samples to a reliable and trustworthy colleague to have an in-depth analysis done. He knew, without question, it would be done off the books and the results would be only between them. He always had a gut feel there was something hinky about Patti's death and he was sure this would provide the proof.

Sure enough, the drugs she had been given were the first ones she had taken. There was a poisonous component that was used to stop her heart seconds after the drug was given. Colin's colleague said that, based on the toxicology, it was most likely given to her in a sports drink and would have been undetectable by her. So, there it was, she had indeed been murdered and it was most likely done by the drug cartel from the case she was working. They were the most likely perpetrators.

Colin had been working on this for quite a while and I was sure his case room at home was already littered with clues and information. He looked at me and said how shocked he was when Norie spoke last weekend about Arturo from La Jolla. He was not yet sure if it was the same guy but there was a connection to Patti's death, and it was a guy named Arturo AND he apparently lived somewhere around San Diego. Everything seemed just a little too coincidental.

I asked Colin if this was all being done outside of work? Was the Bureau aware that he was pursuing other angles? He gave a bit of a dejected smile and said he felt like he could trust nobody at this point. After all, Patti was slipped the drugs that killed her and, at the very least, the coroner was somehow connected.

Obviously, there would have been other people involved in this too.

Coroners do not simply lie about results of a toxicology test on a dead person for no reason. Falsifying an autopsy document can not only get a coroner fired, but they can also end up in jail if it is a serious enough case. People are intense about obstruction of justice these days. Everyone is under a microscope. It is not an area where you want to find yourself dabbling.

Colin went on to tell me that he was using his badge to try to gather information but with the coroner he was nervous about doing so. He then asked if I might consider helping him? He pointed out that I was an imposing presence and could pretend I was anyone I wanted.

There was something in his eyes that made me want to help him. I also knew I was still attracted to him. I was not going to push anything or even move subtly in that direction. I knew I would have to leave it up to him. I did know that I wanted to help him and, by default, help Patti.

He suggested we go back to his house, so we could review what he had so far. We drove over there, and he led me immediately to his case room. As he opened the door I was shocked at the sheer volume of information. The white boards were covered, the walls were covered, there were sticky notes everywhere. There was a ton of information in that tiny, unsettling, and maddening room.

One wall was what we call the structure wall. That is where anyone working in law enforcement, or even doing what I did, typically builds the roadmap of a criminal organization or the blueprint of a crime. It was either an org chart of sorts or a living strategy and planning board.

The structure wall allows one to quickly test different scenarios and as people are discovered, links are made. There were two noticeable dead ends at this point. Arturo and the LA county coroner. Colin said that if I were able to uncover how the coroner was paid, coerced, or threatened to comply, he would work on finding Arturo. We discussed a couple of scenarios and agreed that a simple snatch of the coroner and a very "friendly" interrogation would be the best answer. I was to do this on my own to reduce the chances of Colin being discovered. I agreed.

We had been at this for almost three hours already and it was now late afternoon. Colin suggested we take a break and head out to the patio to have a glass of wine and look at the ocean.

I smiled and said that was always something I could do, almost any afternoon.

He led me out to the patio, grabbing a bottle of wine from his wine fridge on the way out. He poured us each a glass and we toasted to finding the truth.

We just sat in those chairs staring at the ocean for an exceptionally long time, a contented silence enveloping us. The soothing sounds of the waves rolling lazily onto the shore and the light glistening off them was always so relaxing. Each wave telling its own story with me wondering where it started.

We talked about all kinds of things unrelated to Patti's death. As he poured us each another glass of wine, he looked down at me and said it had been tough losing Patti that way, but he was okay now. He said he would always love her but that he had worked with a psychologist and was confident he was moving forward. He was not hell-bent on doing anything crazy to find the guy responsible for killing his wife but if he could, he most certainly would.

He asked about surfing again and reiterated that he would like to meet Duke. I said that I would arrange it sometime for sure. Unexpectedly he then looked over at me and said that he always had a crush on me and asked if I thought that was weird or uncomfortable? I said I didn't think it was and then came clean and told him that I had been attracted to him too, but he was off limits at the time. The whole conversation was not completely comfortable, but it wasn't exactly UN-comfortable either.

Colin said he had always admired my physical condition and that even Patti said that I must be a lot of fun to be with.

I was caught flat-footed by that comment and really had no response other than to smile. Colin said he hoped that didn't sound too strange and mentioned that he and Patti often made comments like that to each other.

He went on to say that he had once watched Jonathon coming down the stairs in his board shorts and caught Patti watching. He looked at her and said that he got it but was happy that she "settled" for him when she could easily have a guy like that. He said they joked that way all the time and it helped them stay closer to one another rather than having the assumed opposite effect. They were both extremely comfortable in their own skin.

He blushed a little when he admitted I was one of his ten "free passes." It was a joke that some married couples have where they admit to each other who they would most like to be with once if that were allowed. I will admit I was flattered by the comment and knew right then we might kiss again at some point.

It would be different from the time I did it at the washroom at Jonathon and Kathy's. That was strictly to throw him off guard and keep him from getting too close to my work with Norie. In some odd way, I felt good knowing that Patti had approved of me, even if only in the free pass scenario. I always liked her and her outlook. She was one of the good ones.

Nothing much more happened this day. We finished our wine and Colin BBQ'd up some steaks and veggies and we had a nice meal on the deck.

It was a really great place, and I knew that I would be on this deck again, hopefully sooner rather than later.

I was already wondering what the others would think about Colin and me together. I was getting ahead of myself, but I would not want to risk damaging my other relationships.

The night ended, Colin walked me out and I Uber-ed home and slept very soundly. I also had an inkling of concern that a relationship with Colin, or anyone else for that matter, might be too much complication in my life right now. After all, I never NEEDED anyone to be happy, I had all the friends I wanted and, thanks to Jonathon and my pension, had no financial concerns either.

Chapter Five – The Coroner Connection

I felt it best to keep the details of my coroner plan to myself. There was no strategic or tactical advantage to Colin or anyone else being made aware of the specifics of what I was about to do. Colin knew I would handle it with discretion, anything added would be extraneous information. The next day I started my surveillance from my home office. I had retained all the equipment I liberated from the government and was unboxing it now and getting everything reconnected again.

It had been more than a year since I had used the gear and I was a little confused, but it quickly became like muscle memory. In no time I was again set up and able to track and watch almost anybody, anywhere, any time. I had the name of the coroner, his office location pin-pointed and his home located. I discovered he lived in the neighborhood just above Hollywood, off Los Feliz boulevard. The area is most notable for it being on the route to the Griffith Observatory, a spot I knew very well. The homes are all quite nice in that area, older Los Angeles style money.

We used to go to the Griffith when I was young. I was always excited because we went up there close to dusk and I knew I would get to stay up late. There would usually be a show going on in the Leonard Nimoy theatre and by the time we emerged, the whole Los Angeles basin had burst into a shining sea of a million lights.

As far as the eye could see lights flickered and shone with the stars above doing the same. Sometimes it felt like I too was one of those stars.

The observatory was like Mecca to me. There was a large centre dome, flanked by two smaller domes all containing high powered telescopes that enabled one to see directly into the heavens. There was always so much to see including the Foucault Pendulum. I never tired of watching it.

The pendulum hangs from the central rotunda ceiling suspended on a 40-foot cable. The orb itself is made of solid bronze and weighs 240 pounds. What makes it unique is the cable is suspended from a large bearing with a ring magnet that allows it to stay in one position. Basically, the pendulum moves in one, constant direction while the building (hence, our planet) turns beneath it.

If I never tired of watching the pendulum it could also be said that I could live in the Oschin Planetarium. It was named after Samuel Oschin, who was born in Detroit but became an Angelino entrepreneur and philanthropist. He loved his new home as much as he loved astronomy and he was always looking to help others. He was a self-made man who gave back constantly to his beloved new home after he became an enormous success. The shows in there always fascinated me and the hosts were so knowledgeable you always left that place a little smarter than when you arrived.

I loved being in the planetarium, seeing and hearing about our planet and all the surrounding stars. Even though it was 290 seats, and they seemed to be all filled constantly, I always felt like I was alone in the heavens. I felt like I was floating through the galaxy seeing everything so close through the lens of the projector.

I sometimes wondered why I never became an astronomer or physicist of some sort. There were times when I was still on active duty that I recalled those days to help me focus, help me work through pain. I even used those images to distract myself from the pain of torture, freeing my mind to plan an escape as I envisioned sitting in that planetarium.

The homes around the observatory are pricey and the ones right on N. Vermont avenue all looked very cool. Most seemed to be character homes and you felt like you were in California in the fifties when you looked at them. I wondered how a Coroner made the cash to afford a place here. I did some sleuthing and found out there was no mortgage on the property but then learned he had inherited the place from his father. That was good, it didn't seem like he was on the take so far.

I watched him and his family closely for a few weeks. He had a lovely wife and three kids, all still school age. The oldest was about to graduate and if the social media feeds I saw were accurate, was going to attend Stanford. A $200,000 education was nothing to sneeze at, so I was back on the corruption angle. I quickly found out she had a full ride golf scholarship and it appeared she would likely graduate from Stanford and head straight to the pro tour. No money worries there either. I kept digging.

Okay, so there was nothing to indicate he was paid off. That meant I would need to explore the threat angle. It wasn't like checking bank accounts, social feeds, or anything else would get me that information. The only way to really do that would be to have a quiet and private one-on-one conversation with him. I couldn't just walk in the front door and ask him either. It would be too dangerous if there was some sort of threat, no matter how I explained myself. Someone could be watching him too.

I recorded his schedule and noted times when he was completely alone. Although not my first choice, I decided I would need to snatch him as he was leaving his office. The place wasn't exactly isolated. The office of the medical examiner is in the Boyle Heights area of Los Angeles, close to the USC Medical Center, East of downtown. The area has quite a lot of history and the microcosm of Boyle Heights explains a good deal about the fabric of Los Angeles.

Boyle Heights was named after an Irishman who purchased about twenty acres overlooking the Los Angeles river after fighting in the Mexican American war.

In the fifties, Boyle Heights was a very ethnically diverse area. Jews, Russians, Serbs, Croats, Portuguese, and Japanese people coexisted peacefully, for the most part. There was not much gang violence back then, everyone pretty much kept to themselves and went about their lives. It soon changed. Freeways began to cut through the neighborhood, sectioning it off, and now it is more than 90% Latino. Not that that is inherently bad, it's simply part of the evolution of the area.

Although the Jews are mostly gone from Boyle Heights, it was not due to discrimination or anything heinous. The banks had begun redlining the neighbourhood. Redlining was how banks identified areas where they would deny home loans. They did not want to risk their money in areas where values had a higher probability of declining. Between that and the freeways, people soon decided investment in the area was a bad idea.

Boyle heights was still an interesting area however, with a lot of history.

Part of that history is the Breed Street Shul, a local Jewish congregation. The Breed Street Shul is in central Boyle Heights. It is listed in the National Register of Historic places. From 1915 to 1951 it was the largest orthodox synagogue west of Chicago. It is also referred to as the Congregation Talmud Torah of Los Angeles. It's quite a building to see and carries in it a lot of history of the area.

Because of these facts, I would need to be mindful of security cameras and knew I would need a disguise. Not too similar to the one I used in my last bit of work when I took out Bobby though. Once I had everything mapped out and knew location and timing, I took some time off to hit a few Wal-Marts and shop for clothing.

Again, I used the clothing to disguise my weight as well as my appearance. I went to other spots and picked up a couple of wigs, various sunglasses, gloves, and other things I knew I would need. Nothing too serious, just enough to scare a coroner a little. Judging by his size and demeanor scaring him would take truly little effort.

I decided I would hide in his own car and wait for him to come out. I would then have him drive to a secluded spot. Once parked, I would cover his head with a hood and explain further what was going to happen. My training had taught me to allow a subject to use his own mind to conjure up worst case scenarios. The THREAT of torture was always far more successful in extracting accurate information than was the actual act of torture. Once you resorted to violence, the battle for the truth was lost. That was why timing was everything when trying to get information this way.

I had a few options of where to go but selected a secluded parking lot up by the Griffith observatory.

I would stash my mountain bike close by, so I could take off quietly down to the base of the hill, load up my bike and drive away. I had the plan ready, now it was simply a matter of timing.

It didn't take long for the right day to come around. I readied myself and confirmed the coroners schedule for the day. I was glad he had his Range Rover as there was lots of room, plus the back windows were completely blacked out. It would be easy for me to hide until I wanted to be seen. I parked my truck and then rode my mountain bike up to a hidden spot and locked it to a tree. I supposed I could have driven it up and done the same thing, but I did not want my truck connected to that location at all. Minor, but a potentially important detail, nevertheless.

I had a bag with me and took a bus over close to the coroner's office after I donned my disguise. I merely sat on a bench in the green space until I got an alert on my telephone that he was on the move. I stayed out of sight of the cameras and slipped into his vehicle through the back door.

I crouched down low and pulled my balaclava tightly over my head and face and waited. I had my voice changer with me as well for added insurance. I heard the door open and the motor start and then we were rolling. Once we got into freeway traffic I sat up on the seat and leaned over the back poking my pistol into his ribs.

I told him his life was not in danger at all unless he chose to speed or break any traffic laws. All I wanted was a little information and he would be released unharmed unless he tried something stupid.

I directed him towards Los Feliz boulevard and told him we were going to take a little drive up to the observatory. I told him I knew he lived close, so he knew where to drive. "Don't make any wrong turns and you will be home for dinner in a couple of hours," I told him.

All I wanted to do was ask a few questions. He blurted out that he did what he asked and now he should be left alone. Well, that was easier than I had expected! I explained to him I was not part of that group but that I really wanted to hear more. He clammed up right away, knowing that he had said something he should not have. His comment confirmed for me there was much more to the situation than met the eye. There was indeed a conspiracy here, now I just had to determine what the connections were.

I directed him to the rear of the parking lot where the spots backed onto thick trees. There were no cars anywhere close and no activity that I could see. The observatory did not usually get busy until closer to sundown.

I also knew there were no cameras in this area, so we had plenty of time to be alone.

I got out of the door on his side and calmly explained we were going to walk quietly into the trees. I told him I was going to put a cloth bag over his head to make sure he couldn't see me at all. I explained this was one more way to help protect his life. He acquiesced and calmly stood as I affixed the bag. I took his hand and led him on our little hike and soon it seemed like we were in the woods in the middle of nowhere, even though we were right on top of the City of Angels. I helped him sit down on the ground and then sat next to him after I removed my own balaclava.

I told him I knew what he had done to the Patti Sharpe autopsy. He began whimpering saying they threatened his wife and kids. They even showed him photos of his eldest daughter and explained how much fun they would have with her. He went on to say that he had absolutely no choice and this was the only time he had ever done something like this. I told him his family was going to remain safe and reassured him that I would tell no one about our conversation.

I only wanted to locate the people who made him do this, but I wanted them for my own reasons. I quizzed him calmly and asked him to remember if he had heard any names mentioned at all. Was there a reference to someone connected? I was probing on many levels in case I could discern either a location or hopefully a name. We had been at it about ten minutes when he said he heard the name Ray used at some point.

They kept saying that he didn't want to disappoint Ray, he told me. A little after that his recall improved and he said, no it was not Ray, it was El Rey. The man who threatened him said he was working for El Rey. I asked if he was certain, and he assured me that he was.

I was recording the whole conversation because I would review it with Colin when we were together. I kept pressing and trying to get any other bits of information that might be helpful, but he had nothing more to offer. I thanked him for his help, reassured him that he and his family would be safe, and then told him to sit still and not move for at least ten minutes. Once ten minutes had passed, he could remove the bag, collect his keys from the ground and then drive off.

He was not to tell anyone about this meeting, not now, not ever. If he did say anything I would do far worse to him and his family than the people who made him break the law. He nodded his head and said thank you, thank you.

I moved quickly through the trees and spotted my bike. I unlocked it, hopped on, and took the short way to the parking lot down through the trees on the dirt path. I had always liked riding these paths and it took me back to a simpler time. I used to ride in here with friends, climbing the paths all the way to the top. We would race to the top; race back down and then go again and again.

I missed those days and sometimes regretted that my life had turned out like it had. I took the time to reflect on the fact that, while I was still doing terrible things, at least I was producing good results. I certainly wasn't the worst person on the planet.

These guys were all guilty. The cops knew it. The victims knew it. Both sides of the legal battle knew it too! The only people who seemed to be oblivious, or too Liberal or too gullible were often the juries. It seemed people could not look past slight errors or missteps to see the true picture. Juries would buy into all kinds of BS stories.

These people were scum and they needed to be put away. As far as I was concerned, I was performing the ultimate public service and that is what helped me sleep at night.

I kept my disguise on even though it was a bit warm for riding. I got down to the parking lot, tossed my bike into the back of my truck and was on the 101 freeway in minutes.

Quick, clean and no witnesses. Just the way I liked it. I believed I had some especially useful information too.

It was a bonus that nobody got hurt, and restored my faith in the system a bit, when it turned out the coroner really had no choice. He certainly was not a bad guy, nor even a criminal, even though he had broken the law.

His family was threatened, and I believe even good people will do dreadful things to protect their loved ones.

Chapter Six – El Rey de los Muertos

Colin and I met at his house later in the week as we had planned. It was a warm day, and I was wearing sandals, shorts, and a tank top. Colin opened the door and smiled, telling me I looked so Californian some days. He chuckled and said other days I just looked like an MMA killer. That one hit a little close to home and I was briefly put off balance, something that does not happen to me often.

I just smiled and said thanks and noted that he was looking rather good himself. As can happen, it appeared he had poured his energy into work and the gym since Patti was gone. He had a dark tan, a hint of gray and a body that could be on TV. Combined with his intellect and attitude he was looking increasingly like a guy I could date. He certainly did not look like your typical fifteen-year FBI guy, with a head full of messy grey hair and a paunch.

I had my recorder with me as we walked through the house. He grabbed a couple of glasses and a bottle of wine on the way and soon we were sitting on that private patio again talking surfing and weather. I told him the meeting had gone smoothly with the coroner, but I didn't really get much.

I explained how his family was threatened and added the comment made about his daughter. Colin completely understood and told me to continue, asking if there were any names at all to go on.

I said Ray but then, just like the coroner did, remembered it was El Rey. Colin perked right up and asked if I was certain? Was the coroner certain he heard the men use the name El Rey?

I explained the context and then queued the recorder up to about where that comment was made. You could hear the fear in the coroner's voice as he told his story. We then got to the part where he clarified what he had heard, and he said it was definitely El Rey. Colin looked at me and asked if I had any idea who that was? I did not, and Colin went on to explain that El Rey was short for El Rey de los Muertos, The King of the Dead.

His real name is Alejandro Flores Garcia. He was called the king of the dead because many, many people seemed to die around him. He was the leader of the Mochismo Cartel. Not mAchismo but rather a play on words because he was often based in Los Mochis, Mexico.

These guys and their names and nicknames still cracked me up. Colin said his was one of the deadliest cartels in the Americas. They would stop at nothing to increase their wealth and spread their influence.

With El Chapo in custody, and the infighting going on within his family and associates, the time was ripe for the Mochismo cartel to step to the top. Even while the Mexican government continued their war on drugs these guys were concurrently having their own turf wars. It was a real firestorm.

Mochismo operates in the Northern Sinaloa district out of a city called Los Mochis. It is a city of around 250,000 so there would be many places to hide, if one felt he needed to hide. Like many of the larger drug lords however, El Rey did not even bother hiding. These guys all felt they were above the law. Most had very senior cops and officials already in their pocket. If they did not own them financially, they had enough dirt on these officials that they lived in fear.

He lives in a fortified mansion close to the coast, almost directly East of Loreto across the Gulf of California. It was a grandiose statement to his wealth and status in the area.

The mansion looked like many others until you got close to it. It was built to withstand bombing as well as ground and even aerial attacks. The dark, steeply pitched reinforced roof and lack of any outcroppings makes an aerial attack extremely difficult. The thick, reinforced walls easily repel virtually any type of projectile or weapon. It truly is a fortress, one that many of the locals know about.

It is claimed it was built to withstand any attack short of nuclear. Had Bin Laden had such a place he would likely still be alive, it was that fortified.

Loreto is in Baja California which, oddly enough, is a Mexican state. I had done some training in Loreto, and even carried out a mission there back in my active days. I remember it quite well. I had always thought it was somehow part of California, even though it was below the Mexican border.

Loreto's location, including its proximity to deep water moorage combined with an airport, makes it handy for drug running and many other illegal activities. Even though Loreto has a population of only 18,535 it has quite a busy airport. It appeared the traffic was mostly criminal, while authorities turned a blind eye. They were no doubt paid off by the wealthy few who run towns like this in Mexico.

The deep-water moorage virtually next door to the airport was always filled with powerful runner-type boats like the Scarab as well as opulent sailing and motor yachts.

The Scarab style boats often had upwards of 1,800 HP being put out by three large V-8's. They were very impressive craft and extremely fast.

The moorage made movement of just about anything to just about anywhere not particularly difficult. Unspoken cooperation by law and port authorities made it all even easier for these criminals to go about their business.

Loreto is also a place of great contrast between groups of people living at opposite ends of the spectrum. It has an international airport but close to it are gravel side streets with people living in cardboard boxes. As you walk towards the water there are million-dollar mansions separated by tiny, unkempt bungalows. The mansions, with six to eight bedrooms and a bathroom for each, likely inhabited by two to four wealthy people. Drug lords and other criminals were the typical owners of these "estates."

The ramshackle bungalows have far too many people living in them and usually two bedrooms with one bathroom. Many of these bungalows had their roofs covered by tarps to prevent leakage and their walls patched with used plywood. These people were living on the very outside edge of life, barely able to feed themselves much less keep a roof over their heads. They toiled as gardeners and cheap labor, doing almost anything for a few pesos.

Even the vehicles illustrated the caste system that has been in place for years here. Sleek and shiny late model Mercedes, Bentleys, and Range Rovers, sitting atop perfectly paved driveways.

Driveways built of decorative pavers and concrete with elaborate patterns built in. Not a rock or speck of dust to be seen on the shiny surface in this most rocky and dusty of places. The vehicles maintained in a constant state of cleanliness by a team of drivers and grooms

In the potholed and eroded gravel or dirt driveway, often right next door, sits older, rusted out and unmaintained pick-up trucks. Their boxes barely able to hold anything due to all the holes.

I recalled driving down those roads and seeing the well-dressed drivers and others lounging in the driveways, the bulge of a weapon not concealed at all by their suits. Some even had automatic weapons hanging from shoulder harnesses, muzzles protruding past the hem of their jackets. This was a real "live by the sword, die by the sword" kind of place. Keeping your head down was a way of life, in some areas the only way of staying alive.

Many times, right next door, a shoeless man in tattered and oil-stained jeans often just watched these dangerous men. I suspected he likely wondered how he might enjoy such a lifestyle. What would he have to do to live like these kings? They were not even aspiring to be the drug lord, they simply wanted to share in a small part of the wealth. For these people, being even the driver would be living like a king. Heck, being one of the servants would be living like a king.

As such, there were many who were willing to do almost anything to improve their station in life. That was exactly what people like El Rey counted on and why they so obviously displayed their wealth. That kind of money can make good people do terrible things. When you have starving children to feed, your moral compass quickly loses its ability to function. Once that line is crossed it is usually behind you forever. The ones who do cross over normally end up dead or in prison.

I looked at Colin and said that he seemed to know an awful lot about this El Rey fellow. He explained that the case Patti had been involved in was with a Los Mochis middleman named Javier Luis Lopez. The confirmation by the coroner told him that the middleman was working on behalf of El Rey and therefore connected to the Mochismo cartel. That was the connection he was seeking. Now, he needed to follow the trail and see where it led.

We practically ran back into the house and straight to his case room where he filled out sticky notes, stuck them on the structure wall and began to connect them with lines. This org chart was starting to take shape.

Colin now knew who ultimately may have given the order to kill his wife. He also had connected it to the middleman. The last, and most difficult step would be connecting everything back to the true source.

The head of the snake. This was the challenge that law enforcement always faced. The leaders were very skilled at insulating themselves from prosecution. These leaders had multiple levels of people, all performing tasks in a vacuum to isolate them.

We talked at length about possible strategies and finding out more about the organization. We needed to connect them to this Arturo from La Jolla fellow and then get close to Arturo. We quickly agreed anything that went at El Rey straight on would most certainly be suicide.

That was when Colin caught me completely off guard.

Chapter Seven – Rogue Mission?

Colin looked me straight in the eye and shocked me with his next words. He asked if I thought that the police, the FBI, even the navy seals would be able to take this guy out. I said none of those organizations were in the business of revenge. They were also unlikely to break the law to this extent unless there was a homeland security angle. DHS opened a lot of doors and made many tactics somehow acceptable these days.

Homeland security was created after nine-eleven and their power and reach now seems virtually unbounded. People, even US citizens, can be held for as long as they want if DHS believes there is ANY connection to terrorism or homeland security. I believe that close to 100% of Americans have no idea what DHS can really do, except DHS themselves. They are most likely doing these things right under our very noses. From black ops sites to psychological and chemical interrogation, I had no doubt that DHS had similarities to what I used to do, only they were now well known.

I went on to share my thoughts on Mexico itself and the level of corruption. I thought it was odd that even though their government declared war on organized crime, it seemed like El Rey operated with impunity. I wasn't totally surprised by this as when I was still active, I completed an op in that area.

I witnessed firsthand exactly how the government, police forces and even the army, cooperated with criminals. Sometimes it was even more than cooperation. I saw cases where the police force themselves were the actual criminal organization and not simply cooperating with one. Those were scary situations. I never trusted anyone during an operation, but this was an added twist.

I think it was due to my training in the region and local knowledge that I was selected for that mission. My Hispanic looks probably helped too. As was my usual method of operating, I was in complete secrecy. I felt sort of like I was in one of those Tom Cruise mission impossible movies, except for the fact I wasn't some shortish, good-looking guy faking it.

I truly was a trained killer and was one of the best operatives in almost any situation. My handler knew I could be counted on to successfully complete any mission. I enjoyed being the best, I aspired to remain the best and that recognition was well-earned. I trained like a fiend, studied like a scholar and did everything possible to improve myself. It was the only way to live that I knew. Be absolutely the best you can be each and every day.

Unlike movies, in real operations there were never all kinds of buildings and vehicles being blown up. It was best when I was never seen, never heard and the target was eliminated covertly. No fanfare, no police.

In my perfect world, the deaths would be interpreted as an accident, just like that poor fellow who died diving off those cliffs. My goal was always to complete my missions with as little flourish as possible and no way to be connected back to the USA.

That was not always the case, because secrecy was not wanted each time. In some operations, the targets were eliminated to send a message. The message being, "don't screw with the USA." If you do, we will hunt you down no matter how or where you hide, and you WILL be eliminated. Look at Osama, he was one of the ones they wanted to be high profile. The message needed to be sent and ST 6 operators did an excellent job of that.

On my mission in that area, secrecy and discretion was absolutely required. I slipped into Mexico and moved quickly to Loreto. I sequestered myself in the sagebrush covered sandy hills and waited, camped out in a camo tent. I had lots of intel but was travelling light so did not have all the gear I would usually carry. I knew where the target lived and had all the details of his security and security people, so I knew when and where.

I determined the how once I reviewed his file in depth. I knew that an air embolus of about 20 ml would kill a person, if injected into the right artery at the right time. The bonus is that it appears to be a heart attack when cause of death is researched. In this case the target was known to be a drug user so one more needle mark was not going to be noticed.

The safest way to get away clean is to immobilize the target with a difficult or impossible to trace drug. My favorite for this is rohypnol, commonly known as a roofie. You can administer it in several ways but hidden in a sweet drink or alcohol is best. The victim doesn't notice anything until they find themselves unable to move. The other benefit is that it cannot be detected via a tox-screen after only 24 hours. It starts to take effect after thirty minutes and around two hours later the victim is usually immobilized.

They are unable to move but cognizant of everything going on around them. Once that was done, it was a simple matter of an air-filled syringe and then time to head North. I inserted the syringe, pressed the plunger, and waited until he was dead.

I completed that assignment and got out of there as quickly as I could.

That was that and now here I was with SA Colin Sharpe talking about the same area. I knew this mission would be much more dangerous. I would not be operating in secrecy and would have little or no support. I would be on my own and out in the public, known by the very people I was targeting. Hopefully, known well and trusted by those same people. Trusted at least as much as these people ever trusted anyone. Trust was in short supply in the middle of two drug wars.

That was when Special Agent Colin Sharpe's words floored me. He leaned forward, clasped his hands together on his knees and with a furrowed brow said that was why he would have to do this on his own.

He was building the intelligence needed to take this guy down, but he knew it would have to be a cold-blooded murder. He also knew that it was likely he too would die but he would avenge Patti's death and that was all that he wanted. That would again make him whole. Whether he lived or died he would be content in having avenged Patti's murder.

I was immediately conflicted as my thoughts raced around in my head like cars in a demolition derby. Opposing thoughts and possible actions crashing into one another and bouncing around in my brain as I tried to remain outwardly stoic. I gathered myself as much as I could and heard myself saying that I loved Patti too and I would help him. I would help him get his revenge. I didn't want him to die and there was no need for that to happen.

He asked why I thought I could do that and, after swearing him to secrecy, I told him a little bit about my prior life. I did not provide a massive amount of detail but when I was done, he calmly shook his head and said he knew I was in such phenomenal physical condition for a reason. He said he hoped that at some time in the future I could share more with him. I made no promises, as bringing someone that far into my world was not a good idea.

Even a seasoned agent like Colin, who had also seen a lot, would likely be unable to compartmentalize what I had done. Those of us who knew each other back in my operations days never even shared every detail.

It was all communicated from a very high-level view. It was simply easier, and safer, that way.

Colin spent the next hour trying to talk me out of helping him. He gave reason after reason why I should stay as far away as possible. I met each with a rational argument, explaining why he needed help and why he needed my help specifically. He may have been a great FBI agent, but I knew, especially fueled by revenge, that he would be no match for these people.

Revenge and the associated emotions always clouded judgement and logical thought. One could easily ignore what would typically be recognized as red flags during an operation.

Revenge was the most dangerous emotion and the largest barrier to success in plays like this. Revenge often got the wrong person killed.

I quizzed him over and over, explaining to him the dangers and how difficult it would be. Once he began coming around to my point of view, I said that we would need to put a long-term plan in place. I highlighted how difficult it would be to get to the top of the organization but perhaps there might be a way.

I provided additional details of my prior life and said that there are usually two ways to build trust and gain access to these organizations. The first is for a woman to find a way to connect with and get close to the head of the snake. I told him that was not the way I operated. Sure, I may have used my gender to get close to someone but never crossed that line, nor would I. I have scruples after all, and I did not have to go that far to accomplish ANY mission. My extensive psychological training gave me all the tools I needed to evaluate any target and determine the best way in as well as what I needed to do once I was in.

I explained that a better and safer approach would be for me to get into the organization and work towards a security/bodyguard type role. He immediately said that was not going to happen. We argued back and forth again and then I laid out for him how easy it is to get in doing it my way.

The guys in the middle, and even at the top of these organizations, are always scared they will be taken out. They spend a great deal of time looking over their shoulder. They eliminate all threats without regard to where or from whom the threat is coming. One day, you're the number two or three guy and the next day you're dead. Killed by your own boss or someone close to him because he thought there was something off about you or your actions.

I went on to explain that is why the bodyguard/security angle is best, especially for someone with my skills. I had the psychological training to be able to get inside anyone's head and have them believe whatever I wanted. I also had the physical training and experience to take care of any obstacle these people might face which would help me move up the ladder quickly.

I would first do something to get me recognized as someone who could help the organization. Perhaps save one of the lower-level guys from death or a beating. That was a safe way, at least it was for me, to get recruited.

We discussed a plan where I would first get in, and then once I did, I would eliminate a mid-level guy. I would kill him and frame him so it would appear that he was indeed working at cross-purposes to his own boss. The killing would quickly eliminate the possibility I was law enforcement. That would be the first hurdle passed, setting me up to move deeper into the organization.

That would also endear me to the bigger boss and help build trust. At least whatever amount of trust could be built with these guys. A typical test of someone is to have them kill an underling or someone else who has fallen from favor. I had no reservations about doing that. A dead crook is a dead crook.

How they got that way, or by whom, was never something that concerned me at any time. It would take a while for us to work out the finer details and these were always fluid situations. One was never sure that a plan would go exactly as drawn up and, in fact, you always had to be prepared for changes.

The changes always came and how you handled them often dictated whether you and the mission lived or died. The ability to be proactive and reactive at the same time was something people like me were trained in. We always had to think four or five steps ahead of the people we were dealing with. I remembered the training in this area and how tedious it seemed but when faced with change, I was always able to turn things back in my favor.

We would leave the in-depth planning for another time as we both needed to relax and have some fun at Kathy and Jonathon's.

Hanging with those guys was now where I felt safest. I sometimes felt guilty I was keeping things from them, but I felt I had no choice. I was sure they all had things about themselves I didn't know.

Of course, none of them could be harboring the secrets I was but still, secrets are secrets.

I was content to love them for who they were, enjoy their company and support them when required. I believed they felt the same way.

Chapter Eight – Party Time

After my conversations with the coroner and Colin I was certainly ready for a little R&R. Anywhere would have done, but I always felt the most at home at Kathy and Jonathon's. I was looking forward to this one. I was also hoping that Sage and Arlo would be there as I felt they may be able to help me with some cartel information. They didn't know anything about the actual cartel, but I knew they were dialed in to the local weed scene and perhaps I might get some actionable intel. Plus, they were a real gas to simply be around.

It was another afternoon start, and by the time I rolled in the place was already packed with the usual suspects. I quickly spotted Norie, Angie & Luke, Arlo & Sage, and a few other familiar faces. I felt a tap on my shoulder and Colin was handing me an ice-cold beer. He said we should down a warm-up beer and then catch a few waves. I said that was a great idea and we began to circulate. It seemed like we always surfed for a bit at these gatherings, and I really enjoyed those times on the water with my friends.

I knew I couldn't just stroll up to Arlo or Sage and ask them about weed, it would look far too obvious. They also would likely figure something was up as they had never seen me smoke it or even talk about it before.

I decided I would approach them because a friend of mine, who wanted to stay anonymous, was having serious health issues. This person really needed pot but had no idea where to get it. She could not take the medical route because she couldn't risk her employer discovering the health issue, or the marijuana use for that matter. It all had to be top-secret.

That was good. My story was ready and now I would just have to wait for the right moment. I was confident that someone in this crowd would table the issue of marijuana at the right time. From there I could easily introduce my plan.

We just hung out and enjoyed some BBQ'd snacks prepared by Jonathon, which were great as always. Everyone was having a fun time when someone noticed the waves were starting to roll in pretty good. About seven of us grabbed surfboards and out we went. Kathy and Jonathon were always so thoughtful. They had prepared every board they own, and each was fully waxed and ready to go. I figured they personally kept the Mr. Zogs sex wax company in business as they likely bought that stuff by the case. I chuckled when I saw the label because I knew all about Mr. Zog.

Mr. Zogs, now there's a great California story for you. These guys make the best board wax and when they started out, Zog was looking for some help branding. He approached a friend of his to first design a label and he, Hank Pitcher, came up with it.

Pitcher wasn't really a branding or marketing guy; he was an artist. But that made him naturally creative, and he used that creativity to brand his friend's company. It was he who came up with the whole Dr. Zog persona and branded everything to that.

When Zog saw the first label design and the name he immediately loved it! It was a cool looking label and logo. The original one was round and caught on very quickly. The sticker had Mr. Zogs sex wax as the main heading, surrounded by phrases such as, "Quick Humps" and "Extra Hard." You can still find those stickers everywhere to this day and the logo shows up on a lot of merchandise. I suspect that the sales of branded T-shirts, mugs, hats, flip-flops, stickers and almost anything else you can brand, brings in far more revenue than the actual product itself.

Although, the wax still sells very well. They have waxes for surfboards including Dream Cream and Really Tacky. They have even diversified and added waxes for hockey sticks and snowboards. I wonder if they plan to develop a wax for people wearing braces to protect their teeth from the wires and brackets? Not sure it would go over so well with parents though. But, like I said, a great California story.

We were all out surfing, and the waves were excellent as usual.

I had found out some time ago that one of the reasons that Kathy and Jon had bought this house was the surfing. Essentially, the house they had originally purchased was long gone. It was the ultimate beach reno.

They built the architectural beauty they now lived in after bulldozing 90% of the house they had purchased. The only part of the original house they kept they had turned into a full-fledged surf-shack that was situated off the side of the middle deck. It was such a cool feature and people often gravitated to that shack. It was a nod to a much simpler time in Socal.

Jonathan and Luke had staked out this part of the beach for a couple of years. They had studied wave patterns, surf reports and all kinds of other information so they KNEW this was where they wanted to be. The only reason Huntington Beach was called Surf City was because this area of beach was all private. It had the best waves; the best breaks and you could get the longest rides right here. If you were intimidated by the huge waves on the North Shore of Hawaii and places like that, then this was the perfect spot. Nice little five to eight footers all day long on most days.

Today it truly was perfection. We were all catching awesome waves. They were even large enough that, if you crouched low on your board, you could sit in the serenity of the tube for what seemed like minutes. In there, you could hear your board swishing over the water, the only sound breaking the silence, as the wave propelled you forward.

There was an eerie calm as you surfed inside the wave, constantly trying to decide whether to turn out, cut back or crest the wave only to race down the face once more. It was beautiful watching the sun shine through the wall of water, bathing the whole inside of the tube in a warm blue-green light. Splashes of salt air and the warmth made you want to stay in there forever. THAT was the danger of the larger and consistent waves!

You sat in there gliding across the face of the wave and every now and then you simply got too calm, too comfortable. That was usually when you misjudged when to turn out or cut back. Or simply forgot. Seemingly out of nowhere, tens of thousands of pounds of water crashing onto your head and forcing you down into the sand. Often you would get driven head-first into the somewhat unforgiving sand and then begin to roll as you tried to get your bearings. Your leash dragged your board along for the ride. If you had the presence of mind, you could follow that leash to the top. Air! But the awesome power of the wave kept spinning you and tossing you around like you were inside a washing machine, spinning out of control, making it difficult to escape to the surface.

The wet suits we wore weren't anything to do with water temperature, they were more like industrial strength rash-guards. I had no desire to display my lack of surfing prowess by running around with all kinds of cuts and scrapes on my arms and legs, or my face.

Those rash-guard shirts could get easily shredded, even though you were usually only hitting sand. I was sure there were rocks mixed in and many times my head verified that fact.

But still, even with a huge crash, the days just didn't get better than this. The warmth of the sun heating you up while it reflected brightly off the waves. Sea spray in your face to cool you off as you rode, twisting, turning, and trying to work with the wave rather than against it. Truly becoming a team for however brief a period, but a team, nevertheless. You and the wave, almost as one. Right up until your teammate did everything possible to make you crash and crash hard.

Still, I could surf, or watch great surfers ride waves, all day. To me it was like poetry in motion, each surfer telling the story slightly differently. Each interpreting the waves according to his or her own skill.

Chapter Nine – Arturo

We had our fill of waves and scrambled back onto shore and showered off. The party was going along quite well. Those who chose to surf had ridden some great waves. Those who did not held down the fort while basking in the sun like seals on a rock. We all now had full bellies and were getting into some serious drinking. I knew that I was staying over so I felt free to consume whatever amount I wished.

Colin and I were sipping on one of our many drinks when Arlo and Sage joined us. As the four of us stood there chatting I hoped I would soon get the information I was seeking.

Arlo sparked up a joint and of course didn't offer either of us a toke. I was a little surprised they would light up, right in front of Colin, but he was a trusted friend and they felt at home with him. I didn't think the FBI ever cared about catching a consumer anyway, plus they both had medical marijuana cards. They knew neither of us partook so it was normal for them just to consume for themselves. For those two, lighting a joint was absolutely no different than us cracking a cold beer. If it weren't so easy to get and smoke pot in California, I figure they would have been moving to Canada soon.

Bit of an odd country that place is. Due to the operation I was on I spent time in Halifax, which is in Nova Scotia, on the East coast above Maine. Very friendly people, who apologize for just about everything. I had been in and out of there a couple of times when I was still in Special Forces and always liked it.

Of course, the Canadian government knew nothing of my excursions, nor did any of their law enforcement folks and that included the world renowned RCMP. Being American, I knew little about their national police force. I came to find out how highly regarded they are while I was there, and some of the things they have done.

The US government knew nothing either. Only my handler knew what I was doing up there. I liked it; it was a great place to visit. Halifax is in the same general region as Gander, Newfoundland. That is the place that helped us tremendously right after 9/11. It is still called an oasis of kindness by those 6,700 people who were helped and taken care of by them. That is more people helped than the entire population of the city!

Their mayor watched the first plane hit the WTC and knew that aircraft would soon be redirected to Newfoundland and his airport. They began preparations, but he had no idea that soon he would have thirty-eight planes parked at his airport. All filled with passengers requiring support, food, shelter, prescriptions, and anything else people needed to live.

All the residents began cooking like mad. The local ice rink, converted to a giant refrigerator, was soon overflowing with casseroles. It makes sense when almost everyone knows everyone else, and people really do not lock their doors. There's even a tony-award winning Broadway musical called Come From Away that tells their story. I'm not sure there is another place like it on the planet. I'd like to go back sometime and just experience the whole place as a regular tourist might.

Pot is not exactly legal in the states but, as one would expect, California leads the charge. Medical marijuana cards might as well be sold like transit passes. The good old Green Doctors. For fifty bucks, on Venice Beach, you could see one of the doctors and get your Med card for just about any condition! I hoped that Arlo would buy my story explaining why I didn't go that route. At their age, and being hippies, they were strong into conspiracy theory, so I felt my story would stand up to scrutiny.

I started to let my story out to Sage and Arlo, and they were listening intently. They offered all kinds of comments on the various strains to tell my friend about and which ones did what. I said that she could not get a med card due to her job and would have to acquire it on the black market. Sage shared that they still maintained some of their contacts from the good old days. They found the potency of some of the medical stuff to be not as good, so they sometimes met with their old dealer. He was now a bit of a bigwig, but he liked them and still let them go to directly to him.

I started to reminisce about the good old days and talked about what a group the old-time dealers were. They came from everywhere and all social classes by the early seventies. That was when Sage mentioned Arturo, claiming he was the best and always had the best product. Bingo! I tried not to jump all over it as I was confident there were many Arturo's around this area. The name wasn't as popular as Juan, let's say, but it was up there.

I played it cool, as we continued chatting, and I eventually got around to asking Arlo if he would take me with him to do a buy.

I said I wanted to meet such a great friend of his and hoped he could convince him to allow that. Arlo explained that Arturo was extremely cautious, especially these days. He said we could likely meet up with him in two or three days. I agreed, and when Arlo said we would have a nice drive down the Coast I was hopeful we would be meeting the right Arturo. We made our plan and then continued partying with everyone.

The party went on well into the night and Colin and I chatted with various groups until things started to wind down. I was about to go to my room when Colin said he was staying around, he didn't want to go home to an empty house. I felt bad for him and said if he got really lonely, he could bunk in with me.

Nothing sexual or anything, just two buds sharing a king-size bed. It wasn't as awkward saying it as I thought, and my only intention was comfort. I knew exactly how he felt.

I also thought it might be good to eliminate the bad karma from Bobby from that room. Everyone said their good-nights and went their separate ways, Colin in the other guest room that shared the bathroom with "my" room. I unlocked the door, stripped down to shorts, and pulled my T shirt back on after ditching my bra.

I climbed into the huge bed and was snoring in minutes. It was so comfortable it was almost impossible to stay awake for any length of time. I have no idea when, but I felt a presence in the bed next to me. I knew it was Colin, so I wasn't worried of course. It was not long after when I felt his body against mine and his hand resting on my hip. I put my hand on his and held it there and I was back to sleep almost immediately.

We woke up in the same position in the morning. I could sense Colin was trying to escape so I just laid there and pretended to be asleep until he was gone. He felt good next to me, and I had some thoughts about he and I, but decided now would not be the best time. I wasn't sure if there ever would be a best time, but I knew it certainly wasn't now.

What we were about to attempt required absolute focus and zero distraction. Muddying the waters with any kind of relationship would do neither of us any good.

I waited what I felt was the right amount of time, got up and went downstairs. There was coffee all around and I was soon ready to face the day.

Chapter Ten – The Buy

The time arrived for Arlo and me to head South. It was a beautiful day to drive down the coast and I was quite pleased that Arlo wanted to drive. He had a gorgeous, perfectly restored Austin-Healey 3000, 1959, I think. They were so sleek and beautiful with their low windowsills, long graceful hood and popped up quarter panels. With the roof down, they were rolling works of art in my eyes. I had always admired them.

It was a gleaming example of the era, a light silver-blue over white two-tone color that was popular at the time. The white started just behind the front wheels and swept back to the rear of car, not unlike the Corvettes back then. It even had the original wire rims. The leather interior had certainly been upgraded but they had matched the original color, which I knew was no small feat. Everything about it was pristine. As we backed out of the garage I smiled when Arlo slipped on one of those British driving caps and even fingerless leather driving gloves.

We pulled out smoothly onto the freeway and accelerated quickly. Obviously there had been some work done under the hood too. I knew the original had nowhere near this kind of power. I chuckled as I looked at Arlo, his long grey hair flowing out from under his peak cap. I asked about the power, and he smiled as he hit the accelerator, while dropping a gear. We shot ahead like we were in a race car.

He explained that, while he loved the vehicle and found it particularly beautiful, he could never really accept the lack of power and torque.

He told me had some minor modifications done. I said there was nothing minor about this power. He came clean and told me knew a bunch of guys from his old racing days and they helped him out a little.

"Minor" modifications turned out to be a complete drivetrain reconstruction that delivered close to Corvette performance. It was pretty much a formula Atlantic motor souped up to the hilt. Twin turbos on the six-cylinder engine mated to a short throw, smooth shifting six speed. It had a clutch and a gear shift handle but there were also paddle shifters hidden behind the steering wheel. This thing was built to fly and fly we did.

I never had so much fun being a passenger in anything except when I got a tour in a navy jet when I was still in the forces. You can't beat those aerial war machines, but this really was a close second for me!

As we rolled further South, I watched the signs and was happy when we exited the freeway into La Jolla. Once we were off the freeway Arlo told me to let him do all the talking. He said we were going to Arturo's house and that he was one of only a few people that were allowed to do that. I was surprised he was even allowed to bring me with him.

We were clearly in a nice neighborhood as we drove past street after street lined with huge homes and almost-mansions. It still amazed me how lucrative the drug business could be if one was willing to accept the risk.

We slowed down and turned onto a short street. At the end was a large home with a locked gate. We pulled up and the video screen on the post came to life. A rough voice welcomed Arlo asking where the "son-of-a-bitch" had been. Arlo said he was just doing his thing and the gates swung open admitting us.

We pulled through the heavy-looking iron gates, around the house to the back and parked in one of eight spots. The rear of the house was perhaps even more amazing than the front. There was a massive, gleaming blue infinity pool and a huge tiki bar complete with thatched roof. There must have been at least a dozen stools around the bar, and it was equipped with three TVs, so every spot could see what was playing.

We walked over to where he sat, and I was introduced as an old and dear friend. Arturo extended his hand and said, "I am Arturo from La Jolla." I held in a laugh, thinking it can't possibly be this easy, can it?

As instructed by Arlo, I kept quiet as he laid things out for Arturo. He must trust Arlo an awful lot as he didn't even ask if I was a cop or anything like that, just a bunch of really broad questions.

I had $500.00 bucks on me but kept it out of sight, not knowing how they worked. I did not want to spook him or get Arlo into any trouble. After a little more chit chat Arturo asked what the contribution was. Arlo looked at me and said five small and Arturo said that would be no problem.

Pick up would be as usual and the deposit would also be made as usual. Arlo just said thanks and I like your style. Arturo smiled and said it really was great to see Arlo again, it had been far too long. Someone brought out three drinks and some snacks, and I sat there like a bump on a log as the two of them caught up. It seemed like they had known each other forever.

Finally, they shook hands, Arturo thanked us for our kind donation, and we got back into the car. Arlo handed me an envelope and told me to write the number five on it and add my initials. As we drove around the other side of the house to exit, we stopped at a small shrine. It was a Spanish looking religious statue complete with a small fountain and a slot for "donations." You saw lots of these around San Diego, so it wasn't out of place at all.

Arlo took the envelope from me and dropped it through the slot. We pulled ahead further and there was an opening in the shrubbery on our left. It was the property next door and next to the driveway, completely enclosed in a canopy of year-round greenery, was a small metal box. Arlo opened the door and pulled out the package inside. It was wrapped like a gift box of candy.

Before we pulled away, he lifted the lid, ate one of the chocolates, and then checked out the bottom compartment. That was what held the purchased product. He said everything looked great and out the gates we went.

I had no idea who they thought they were fooling but I did like the setup. As we drove back, I tried to extract additional information from Arlo about Arturo, and he was quite forthcoming. He said that this was some of the best pot in California and it came straight from Arturo's friend in Mexico.

He said Arturo's friends had a few nice boats that they liked to take sportfishing and perhaps drop the odd parcel with a radio tracking device on it every now and then.

They could still be coming from anywhere, but I was hoping his "people" were Mochismo, or someone connected to them. I made a crack that I hoped it wasn't El Chapo or this might be the last we see. Arlo said Arturo would never deal with that scumbag and besides El Chapo was back in custody. He laughed and asked if I lived in cave or something?

In case this was the right Arturo I had left behind a couple of electronic devices. One of them would allow me to identify his local area network so I would know when I was tapped into the correct one. I was now eager to get back home and get started.

The best way to determine his connections would be to follow the money and the dope. These guys could get careless online when they think their networks are un-hackable.

Of course, no network is un-hackable and that was proven in the recent election. Whether our President colluded with anyone or not should be of less concern than if the Russians, or anyone else, can get inside our systems! That was a worry for another day though, so I pushed it out of my mind.

The drive North was just as great as the one South except for a little more traffic. Arlo drove that thing like a race car though, so traffic had negligible impact. He seemed completely unconcerned that, medical card or not, we had five hundred bucks' worth of black market weed with us.

We pulled up to his place, I thanked him and jumped back into my car after grabbing the box of "chocolates." I had to restrain myself as I wanted to floor it, so I could meet with Colin and then get home and get set up.

I was at Colin's house in no time, and we went directly to his situation room. We added a few more connectors and agreed that we would just lay low while I did my work.

We talked about the possible danger to Arlo and decided we should think about how to handle that aspect. He asked me about this Arturo fellow, and I explained that he did not look like anything special or out of the ordinary.

He didn't look at all dangerous either but looks can quite deceiving in some of these cases.

Chapter Eleven – Stage Two

When I got back to my home office, I immediately got things up and running. Thanks to the device I had left in the yard of Arturo I had only three networks to check. I laughed at the stupidity when I saw a network named Artlj. Really?? Arturo from La Jolla named his network with his own initials.

I got my intrusion program running and was quite surprised at how long it took to gain access. He had almost government level security. I suppose that was why he wasn't worried about the name. I found that people like him often felt they could operate with impunity, that even if they were caught nothing would stick. Often, that was exactly what made them vulnerable.

I checked the system every fifteen minutes or so and finally, after way more time than it should have taken, I had access. I set up a few keywords in the search engine that would monitor the network for me and alert me when they surfaced. Words like package, El Rey and some others were my initial setup. Now it was time to watch and listen and begin tracking what was happening.

I first needed to confirm with certainty this was the right Arturo and then I could begin planning the next phase. I had no idea how long this would take but I was prepared to wait. Turned out I didn't have to wait long as a couple of communications mentioning ER quickly showed. When I read them, it became clear that ER was indeed El Rey.

One of his men had communicated to Arturo that ER felt tomorrow would be a perfect evening to go fishing. It was obvious that fishing meant fishing for the packages they usually drop for pick up. I had retained a lot of the information acquired during the operation that I ran in this area, so I gathered that up and got ready. I had some maps and other things that could help.

I met with Colin and discussed my plan. I would let a small group of petty criminals know about the drop and the boat that Arturo, or more likely his men, would be on. I would provide an approximate location and time for the pickup. The bozos would board a lightly protected boat thinking they were going to have an easy time, grab some drugs and get out.

I would pose as a broken-down pleasure boater with Colin. I would board their boat in hopes of getting a ride to shore for fuel and then take out all the bad guys, leaving Arturo with a perfect story to tell his mates. Because they were engaged in illegal activity, they would not want to raise any red flags by NOT helping a fellow boater, so I was confident they would stop.

It would be pure coincidence that I happened to be there so soon after buying drugs from him. That could be my way in. He might get suspicious but when you virtually save someone's life, that eliminates a lot of suspicion.

The plan was set, and I believed it would be effective and get me the "in" I was seeking. Now it was only a matter of execution.

Chapter Twelve – Executing The Plan

I didn't have a lot of time to get the plan moving. I contacted a group I knew would be interested in an "easy" drug heist and left the information with a go-between. Maintaining some of the contacts from my old life sometimes came in handy. I didn't know for sure if they would take the bait, but I was hopeful. At that level they typically aren't all that intelligent and someone tossing them a freebie was usually accepted at face value.

We took a rental boat out as we thought that might be more convincing for a mechanical failure. We motored out about three miles from where we knew the drop may occur and set up my remote tracking gear to search for signals. It was starting to get dark already so the antennas, if visible at all, would resemble fishing rods if anyone got close enough to look.

I located the signal about two hours later and we allowed time for them to pick up the package. Whether the crooks boarded their boat before or after we arrived was not critical, but I thought it would be better if we were already on it. We zipped closer, ensuring we would be almost directly in their path. We cut the engines and raised our boater in distress flag and shone the light on it. A flare could scare off the crooks, so we didn't want to go that route.

Sure enough, they motored over closer to us when they spotted the flag. We said our motor died and asked if they could tow us in. Colin was still inside at that point. They tossed me a longer heavy-duty rope, we connected the two craft, and then we climbed onto their boat. There were only two of them as I expected. We were about seven miles out by my reckoning, and I was really hoping that the crooks were going to show.

Just as I was beginning to lose hope, I saw a dark shape on the horizon. The boat came up on us quickly and suddenly there were bright lights shining in our eyes and people screaming. There were four armed men that I could see. They boarded the boat quickly and took the guns away from the pickup men. They used zip ties to cuff the men. Oddly, they didn't tie me up. I suppose they weren't worried about me, after all, I was just a woman. I loved it when I had their own ignorance and misogyny acting in my favor.

I watched and waited for my chance as we moved slowly through the water. They sent one guy in to search for the drugs and left three on deck. My chance came when one other was summoned to help. That left two on deck and I was ready. I needed to disarm them with no shots being fired so I would wait for them to get close to each other and then make my move. I was seated on the side of the deck when they got a little too close for their own good.

I struck upward with a vicious shot straight into the guy's groin. When he doubled over in pain, I knocked him out with a hard strike to the side of his face. I may have broken his neck, but he was, at the very least, out cold.

Before the other guy could react, I grabbed him and flipped him overboard, disarming him before doing so. I knew where we were, and he would be shark food in short order, if he didn't drown.

Drowning was more likely though, as sharks didn't exactly hunt for humans, although they are opportunistic eaters.

I left the other guy tied up so when the other two came up they would not see anything out of the ordinary. I crouched on top of the roof right above the steps and waited for the two others to come out. I disarmed them both, tossing their guns over the side, but was unable to disable them immediately so now the fight was on. I ensured that it was short and brutal, and it was. I got beside one after striking the other directly mid-chest. He was in pain on the deck and gasping to try to get a breath.

His friend took a not-too-bad swing at me for which he earned himself a painfully broken arm. After I twisted and shattered his bones, I flipped him by the head as he yelled out. A strong grab, firm twist and he was done. His thick neck fairly easily broken.

The other one was ready to go again and, although difficult to do on a boat, I disabled him with a roundhouse kick to the head.

He had no idea it was coming and didn't see it until I shattered a few bones in his face. As he staggered, I struck directly up into his nose with an open palm and that was it for him.

I untied the three men. Colin was a little surprised and the other guys could not believe what they had seen. I told them we didn't care one bit what they were doing or what the deal was, we just wanted to get to shore and return this piece of crap boat we rented. They thanked me and grilled me about what I did for a living and for whom I worked. I told them I didn't work and left it at that.

Before we landed, I left them a few breadcrumbs after they said their boss would surely want to reward me. I knew that being TOO available was dangerous and playing hard to get was the best approach. Not too hard to get of course, it was always a balance when you played that game.

We landed on shore, thanked them profusely and knew it would now be a waiting game. I felt that of the information I gave them the most likely place they would connect with me would be the gym. I would not use a place I did frequent in my regular life, so I selected a different gym at which to become a regular. I had been training there for almost eight weeks now so was already getting well-known, which is precisely what I wanted to happen.

I continued with my regular routine, ensuring I was at the gym close to the same time every day. It took longer than I expected for them to contact me after my display of murderous prowess on the boat. Finally, I was in the middle of doing some heavy squats when I recognized one of them up at the front.

I glanced up there and gave him a chance to make eye contact, which we did. He smiled and waved at me, and I waved back as I walked towards the front. We walked over toward the juice bar, and he said that as he mentioned, his boss wanted to thank me.

I smiled and said they had rescued us. All I did was pay back that favor. We were grateful they took the time to stop and help us.

He looked at me and said their boss wanted to both thank me and meet me. They were always looking for good people to associate with. The hook was in, soon I would be reeling in the next largest fish.

Chapter Thirteen – Small World

I agreed that I would meet them and asked when they were thinking. I was shocked a bit when they said he is waiting outside right now. Most times I would not put myself into a situation like this, but I felt if I tried to hold him off that it would look suspicious. TOO hard to get and they would just disappear, and this was a one opportunity deal. I decided I needed to meet him now, even though I had no backup close.

I told them I needed to shower and change and, being cautious criminals, they said I was fine the way that I was. Good move on their part. They left me no chance to contact anyone, no possibility of setting a wire and no opportunity to get a gun. If I put up too much argument, they would no doubt become suspicious. I suppose they may not be quite as dense as they seemed.

We walked together out the doors into the bright sun where I was led to a waiting black, tricked-out Escalade SUV. I suppose they figured if they were good enough vehicles for SWAT and the FBI, they were good enough for them. This one looked fast even while it was parked with larger rims, lowered chassis, and dark windows everywhere. I would bet those windows were bullet proof too.

The one grunt opened the door for me, and I stepped in. Arturo was sitting on the other side. I reached out to shake his hand and when he shook mine, he looked me in the eye and said, "you're Arlo's friend aren't you?"

He had a serious look on his face when he said it, so I laughed it off and said what a small world it was. There was no way he could know that anyone had hacked his network and my boating story made complete sense. I just needed to stick to the storyline. I flinch, I could die. With a population of more than thirty-nine million in California I found it bizarre that he could think this was a coincidence, but he seemed to believe it. Of course, I now noticed the two men in the third row, each with a gun pointed at my head.

I had purposely not created an alias or backstory to cover the operation. My home, bank account and everything else was completely isolated from me so I had no worries there. I felt that, with their organization and reach, it would be best if I stuck with my true story. It would easily explain them being unable to gather background information on me and it would help me sell my need for cash.

After all, military and government jobs do not pay that well. They usually have okay pensions but that's about it. It would also help explain my skills and talents. It was a risky way to go but, as Thomas Jefferson said, "with great risk, comes great reward."

He looked different somehow. It could have been the glass or the rougher demeanor he was displaying, I couldn't put my finger on it. I smiled at him and asked if we really needed the two gunmen in the back when all he wanted to do was thank me?

He explained that from what he had heard about what happened on the boat the two men with guns and two others outside might not be enough to protect him. He knows of no females, and very few males if any, that could so easily disarm four armed men.

I met his steely stare with my own, smiled and said I supposed that was true. I added that, if I had wanted to cause trouble, it would be down to only him and me already. He softly said he was fairly sure that was the case and he really just wanted to thank me. He said that I had saved his men from getting blown up on the boat and that the thieves were messing with the wrong people. He pulled an envelope out of his jacket and said that he was grateful for my help.

I folded the envelope and tucked it into my shorts and thanked him for his generosity. We shook hands once more and he added that his men might drop back in sometime to see if I wanted some work, if that was okay with me. I told him it might be as I disarmed both men in the blink of an eye.

I tossed both weapons towards the vacant front seats and as I locked up the one arm I smiled at Arturo and said please tell your men not to ever point a weapon at me again. The next time I won't be so gentle. Neither looked particularly thrilled with me but Arturo had a hint of a smile as he told me I too should be careful. As the door opened for me, I explained that I always was.

I strolled casually back into the gym to finish my workout, but I stopped at my locker to check out the envelope. The envelope was thick, so I knew there was a decent amount in there. I was still shocked to see a one hundred pack of crisp one-hundred-dollar bills. $10,000 for saving his men and, of course, his shipment. Well, well, crime did pay.

Of course, with my pension, inheritance, and my growing investment account, thanks to Jonathon, I didn't really have any money worries.

I decided I would use the money for charitable causes, and whatever other cash I was rewarded with I would do the same. There were a great many to choose from but the one closest to my heart was the Wounded Warrior Project. They provide support including programs, services, and events for wounded veterans. They help current and former service people suffering from physical and emotional trauma and help us all live better lives after serving our country.

Whether physical injuries or afflictions like PTSD, veterans can get the help they need in addition to whatever the VA provides them. It is a noble cause and one which I have always admired and supported. If we cannot support and care for the very people who allow us to live the lives we enjoy, then there is something seriously wrong with our society.

I will have to spread out my donations and give them anonymously of course, but I am fine with that. I know they will put this money to great use.

Chapter Fourteen – Background Check

So, the plan was now in motion. I thought it started quite well but realized it may have been a little over the top for me to have disarmed his two goons. I supposed I would see how that played out as we moved ahead. It could even work in my favor and help me move up the ranks quicker. It could also put me in a bad spot with the two henchmen so I would have to keep an eye on them both.

I knew they would commence some deep background checking on me now and I assumed their connections would help them. I stayed away from all my friends during this time and only met Colin at his house. I knew how to ensure I was not followed, and thanks to my own electronic gear, there was no way I could be bugged or tracked. I had jammers and devices that could make it look like a GPS tracker on my vehicle was hundreds of miles away. Our government had developed some great toys for people like me.

I had been driving my truck to the gym and I chuckled when my detector went off, alerting me there was a device transmitting my location. I knew this would happen and I was prepared for it. I had to make sure they thought the device was working fine and they knew where I was frequenting. I would leave the gym and head directly to a large condo complex where it would be difficult for anyone to follow me.

Sometimes I would change in my truck and slip out the back way onto the beach path and go for a nice long run. I always enjoyed oceanfront running.

The temperature was cooler, and the moist air always felt good in my lungs. I could run right close to our houses if I chose and that was good too.

I had rented a parking stall in the complex under my own name. The stalls were not connected to actual addresses, and they were scattered everywhere. I had an underground stall where I also kept a motorcycle. I had purchased a new sport bike as that way I would look at home in a full-face helmet and could easily disguise myself. My old Hayabusa was a 1300 CC rocket on two wheels, capable of over 190 mph before any modifications. It was the fastest bike on the planet when it first came out.

I loved that scoot but my new ride, the Ninja H2R was capable of slightly over 240 miles per hour! I also liked the way it handled. While one might never twist that throttle all the way it was good to know you could be faster than anything on the road, and even most helicopters in the air. Plus, it wasn't as obvious as Ducatis and other look-at-me punk bikes. It was quieter than most and handled well too. Nothing more than bucketloads of somewhat understated power and torque.

So, I kept up the charade for a while. Driving back and forth from the condo complex to the gym.

I would blast out on my motorcycle every now and then and visit Colin at his house to discuss plans. He was taken aback when I told him about my first encounter with the "boys," but he had calmed down since then. I suppose after watching me demolish four armed men on the boat his confidence level increased.

I was beginning to grow weary of waiting for my next contact, but I knew that was my only play to ensure I remained above suspicion. Finally, after more than six weeks, the boys showed up at the gym again. This time they waited outside until I was finished and were leaning against my truck as I came through the doors.

It was the two who had originally contacted me and not the two I had disarmed. I was glad for that. It could have been a little awkward if it were the two gunmen, what with me being female and all that sort of thing!

We stood and chatted briefly, and they asked if I had given Arturo's offer any consideration? I said that I had and, depending on the opportunity, I was interested. They added I would be paid five times what I received in the first envelope; Arturo is very generous with his people.

I asked what the job was and what I would have to do. They said I had to agree to the cash first and then they would take me to him where he would describe what was needed. I said it would really depend on what the job was and that was all I could say. They smiled and said that Arturo said I would probably say that, and I should just get in the car, and they would take me to him.

I got in the car and sat quietly as we drove across the city and entered an industrial area. I was concerned but I had gotten myself in much worse situations than this.

I remained at the ready and prepared for anything.

Chapter Fifteen – The Warehouse

We drove up and parked amongst many other cars, next to the black Escalade. The door opened, and I was asked to get in, so I could speak with Arturo. He started by saying that he was impressed at our last meeting, especially the way I disarmed two of his best men. He said they had been trying to explain themselves ever since and he was tired of it.

He went on to tell me that, in his organization, nothing was handed to you. You had to compete and work hard for everything you earned. I told him I was no stranger to challenging work. He said that his organization was similar to an orchestra. If one were the first violinist, you could be challenged by the second or third chair at any time.

They would be given a piece of music which both would play. Each would be evaluated as they played. The victor would either retain his or her position as first chair or the challenger would seize it from them. This was the way to ensure the cream was always at the top. He looked at me and asked if I wanted to challenge for first chair? I said I did and when would we start.

He said my challenge was waiting inside. I walked through the door to see a cage set up, chairs all around and about fifty people.

I watched as two people worked through the crowd, apparently taking bets. Large bets by the looks of the stacks of cash. So, his "first chair challenge" was also a fight club. Fantastic way to make extra money I supposed. Not my kettle of fish but I wasn't completely against it. I turned to him and said I would be more than willing to meet his challenges, but I would never again participate in such a venture. I told him if he wanted me to go ahead that he needed to agree to that. I added that he would not be disappointed. He nodded his agreement.

I was led to the ring and not at all surprised to see TWO men enter the cage. They did not look happy, even more upset than when I disarmed them in the SUV. Luckily, there were no weapons that I could see but there were no guarantees that none would materialize. I stretched out and warmed up outside the cage and then slowly stepped inside when they were on the other side.

There was no referee, just the three of us. The cage was closed and locked behind me and we started circling. They spread out on each side of me in an effort to distract me, each one jumping around and pretending to move in close and then backing off. I simply stood there, not responding or even flinching as they played around. It must have looked quite odd to the crowd.

They were large, and they were strong, but I was not at all concerned. I had taken out larger, stronger, and faster men who were much more dangerous than these clowns. But it is never good to underestimate your opponent, so I took the measure of each as we all circled the cage. The one had obviously had knee damage at some point in his life. His left knee was shaped a little differently than his right, likely scar tissue.

I saw no obvious fault with the other one. I hoped he would be the second one in. Or if they attacked at the same time, that he would perhaps lag behind the other. I was so focussed, I didn't even hear the crowd, just a pounding in my head as the adrenalin coursed through my body. Every nerve on edge, every muscle twitching, my eyes darting back and forth while my body remained in ready position.

Finally, they came at me. I didn't want to encourage this fight club crap, so I wanted to take them both out quickly. They were staggered the way I had hoped and when they got close enough, I made my first move. I lunged at the first one and used his head as a pivot allowing me to deliver what should have been an almost-fatal kick to the head of the one lagging behind. He fell back spitting out blood as he went, and I continued around on the first guy and ended with a kick directly to the side of his compromised knee.

He screamed and went down in a heap as his knee exploded inward. The kick was perfectly placed. I knew it had at the least, dislocated his kneecap and likely torn all the connective tissue. As I came back to ground and watched him grab the fencing to support himself, I was shocked to see the other one coming at me. His face was a mess. I would think I may have broken his jaw and he certainly had fewer teeth than when he started. I was stunned to see him coming back at me.

One thing I always remember is that no matter how big, how fast, or how strong someone is, the knee is a fragile and poorly designed joint. It was the simplest and quickest way to take down someone, especially when they were of larger stature. The remaining knee had to hold all that extra weight.

No matter how much you trained, how often you lifted weights, and how limber you were the knee was always a weak spot.

As the other held himself up on the cage I positioned myself for this guy. He kept coming at me with murder in his eyes. I had to let him close, or my kick would do no good. His arms were longer than I expected, and he now had one on my throat as he cocked his other arm to punch me. I was not about to take an almost open shot from a guy that size!

Before he could unload, my foot crashed directly into the front of his knee, collapsing it backward. You don't have to be a Doctor to know that is not the way the knee is designed to bend.

He went down hard screaming in pain. Now it was almost comedic watching the two of them, each one standing on one leg. Honestly, I could not believe they were able to stand at all knowing the pain they were in. I had seen tougher men pass out after receiving a kick like the second one.

I figured it was over when I looked out at Arturo as I walked toward the gate. I was shocked to see him give the thumbs down, Julius Caesar style. I knew then if I didn't finish them, I would likely be done myself. Scenarios ran through my mind as quickly as I could process them, but I saw no option. I had no choice but to kill them both. Apparently, it wasn't good enough just to beat the first violinist in Arturo's orchestra, you had to completely eliminate him.

One came at me, hopping on one leg and attempting to grab me.

I had no desire to torture these poor buggers so when he was close enough, I unleashed a brutal strike up into his nose. I put all my power behind the punch, and I was certain I drove bones and skull fragments up into his brain. He went down in a heap, and I was certain was dead not long after he hit the canvas.

The other was still using the fence for support. As I approached him, he began to swing wildly at me. On one swing I was able to secure his arm and twist as I moved in behind him.

I now had him in a choke hold with my arms holding his own arm tightly against his neck. I could feel him begin to weaken quickly as he struggled for tiny gasps of air. I arched my back and lifted him off the ground as I drug him away from the fence all the while tightening the hold. I knew if I quickly twisted the other direction, I could snap his neck and his pain would end so that was exactly what I did. I let him drop as the crowd gasped and then everything went silent.

I exited the ring, escorted by Arturo's other guys without a mark on me. These guys were way overmatched, I knew that. The bettors clearly did not. They could have had weapons and they would have still been out of their league. I felt bad but then I knew I would have to do terrible things to move up the ranks. Besides, I was certain these creeps had killed not-so innocent people as well as innocents during their day-to-day activity.

Arturo shook my hand and said welcome to the team. We went out to the car and had a drink as we waited for the men to come out. The driver got in and when the passenger got in, he handed two envelopes to Arturo. Arturo asked if it was half and half and he said he checked it twice.

He put one in his jacket and handed me the other saying it was likely more than fifty thousand as the betting was fierce. He said, apparently women like me are exceedingly rare.

It was thanks to me that he won big, and we were splitting the take fifty-fifty. I thanked him and put the envelope in my pocket. He asked if I was going to count it and I said I wasn't too worried. We drove in relative silence back to my truck until Arturo finally said that he needed a new security person. He would maintain his two bodyguards, but I would be the insurance policy. I would be the one watching everyone's back and ensuring that if there were any internal issues they would be handled.

He said the job paid $7,000 per week and there might be opportunities to make even more than that. I thought more than 350K a year wasn't bad cash for this kind of thing, especially as I wasn't exactly the front-line person. We shook hands and I said that he had his man, so to speak. That made him smile a wry smile and gave me a good laugh too.

The plan was working and working very well thus far. Maintaining vigilance was now more important than ever. These guys could be spooked by just about anything. I was now in the equivalent of deep cover and would need to make sure that I was on my game 100% of the time, never letting my guard down.

The advantage for me is that I KNEW I could never trust any of these people, they did not have the same perspective. These were simple psyches to manipulate.

Sure, they didn't really trust anyone but after my display I knew they would become much less vigilant.

Chapter Sixteen – Living Arrangements

I drove down to the house the following day to have a look around and discuss the job a little further. It was a busier drive than I expected as heading South at this time of day should have had less traffic. The lines of traffic travelling North on I-5 always amazed me. A seemingly solid wall of steel and tires moving inexorably Northward. I supposed that it was now like this all the time in both directions, Angelinos driving South to work and Southerners driving to LA and the surrounding area.

I pulled up to the gate and was immediately recognized and buzzed in. I drove slowly around back and parked where I parked when Arlo and I were here. As I got out of my car, I was searched for a weapon by one of the guys. I watched Arturo smiling as I told his goon that I didn't need a weapon to take him out, so he should watch where he puts his hands. He was indeed careful not to go near any sensitive areas when they normally would go there first.

This was good. I had the respect, or perhaps just the fear, of the men already. I really did not care which one, although I preferred fear to be honest. Fear can make an opponent do things he would not normally do, which creates openings for me. In a fight, fear can make people attempt things out of desperation and anything other than a perfectly executed mov
e against me, was destined for failure.

We sat in the warm California sun, gazing out at the ocean, as Arturo gave me a little more information. It was completely focussed on him and his security needs. There was no discussion of his "job," if that is what we are going to call it. He said that, after watching me first disarm his two gunmen, and then destroy them in the ring, that he knew he needed me on his team. He said he found out a lot about me and was glad I had military training.

I had created a profile that supported my story and it appeared I was just another army grunt who worked hard and got ahead. There was no connection to my real special forces work, as all of that remained inaccessible to anyone.

He said that I could live wherever I wanted but I could have my own room and quarters in the attached guest house if I preferred. I said I would think about that as renting a condo was costly where I lived. I knew he was aware of where my parking space was, and those condos were pricey. I also knew that closer would be better if I was to learn about the organization, share information with Colin, and continue with our plan. It wasn't like we were ever going to court so the method of gathering intelligence was inconsequential. I could break all the rules and privacy laws that I wanted.

Arturo summoned one of the men to show me through the house. There was a living-quarters that looked like part of the main house but was entirely separate, except for one hidden door. As we walked through the main house, I spotted cameras everywhere. They tried to hide them, but I knew exactly where to look.

The house itself was a work of art, curved walls, and curved glass everywhere that provided an amazing view up the coast and out to the open ocean. The design was such that the inside and outside seemed to seamlessly blend together, joined only by vast expanses of marble and stone floors.

The spaces were separated by huge glass walls that could retract into the outer walls, making outside and inside even closer to being one space. Due to the curves and connection to the environment It appeared it was designed by Frank Lloyd Wright as a nod to the Guggenheim. I couldn't help but think how much Kathy and Jonathon would like this house, except for being a little too far from the best waves.

Even the pool and spa were large, curved works of art. The infinity pool provided a perfect view of the Pacific. The house was elevated as well so it was easy to see anyone approaching, whether they were on the road or traversing the land. The landscaping was created to isolate the house and provide an open buffer-zone to easily spot any intruder.

He said Arturo would give me the full tour when he discussed his schedule with me, and we went into the kitchen pantry.

At the rear on one side, he grasped one of the shelves and lifted it up, revealing a door to the other side. He explained that the guest house was constructed as a panic room. It was basically built into the stone beneath the house and, if there was trouble, it offered perfect protection. Once locked down there was no way in or out, except for the panic tunnel.

The walls were bomb-shelter thick reinforced concrete, the air supply was self contained and water came via an underground spring.

This section was completely self contained and one could live sealed-up in there for as long as six months. Except for one area, which I was sure was Arturo's, this section was all utilitarian. There were no marble floors or massive expanses of glass and tile or huge walk-in showers. The floors were a terrazzo style concrete, and the kitchen resembled a commercial one. Gleaming stainless steel and equipped with a huge walk-in freezer and cold room. The only nod to opulence was the extensive wine storage and tasting room. It wasn't so much the style that was opulent, it was the huge quantity of what I knew were expensive wines and scotch whiskies.

He showed me a couple of the rooms, including the one which would be mine. Again, utilitarian in nature but still lacking nothing.

Each room was its own little enclave with a private bath and shower, large closet, and a comfortable sitting area with a massive TV. There were eight such rooms in here.

In addition to the kitchen, there was also a shared area that included sofas and those reclining drink-holder chairs around what looked like an 80-inch TV. He said the boys liked to watch football and other sports and often they all did that together.

Obviously, it would be much more difficult to get any private time at all if I lived here. I suspected we would also be cut off from the outside as far as cell service went. I had to come up with something quickly to allow me to keep in touch with Colin. I also had to get some of my more discreet equipment inside in case I needed it. Much of it was already well disguised so I did not anticipate a problem. I thought it unlikely he would be prepared for an intrusion by someone as well equipped as I was.

We finished the tour and returned to the poolside area. It was now close to noon and I was wondering why I wasn't seeing any women around. As if on cue, a couple pulled up in a convertible Lamborghini. As they stepped out it was impossible not to notice they looked like high fashion bathing suit models, only curvier. They both appeared to be Hispanic and were tall, dark, and stunning.

As they walked towards us, I instantly felt a little less womanly. I couldn't help it, every now and then I was challenged by those feelings. Even my shrink could not help me understand why.

They went to each side of Arturo and gave him a peck on the cheek. They clearly knew their station as they did not ask about me and barely acknowledged that I was even there at the table. He chose not to introduce us either and suggested they go for a swim; he would join them shortly. I watched as the two long-legged beauties walked slowly to the edge of the pool, kicked off their shoes, removed their dresses and dove in.

They seemed to be wearing the same black, one-piece bathing suits. I didn't know if I was in a James Bond movie or a Robert Palmer video, but I found the whole situation a little surreal. Arturo looked at me and said that most women were clearly not as talented as I was, but they had other skills. I just smiled at him and said that I supposed they did.

He asked if I liked the tour and if I wanted to take advantage of the living arrangements. I said that it seemed like the best idea plus I could save even more money. Before officially moving in, I told him that I needed to understand exactly how this worked. I explained that I wanted to continue training at my own gym. I knew the drive up and back would give me talking time and being in my own gym would be a terrific way to facilitate communication with whomever I needed to speak with.

He asked if I had seen the gym in the staff house and I said I preferred to interact with regular people. I told him it helped keep me prepared. He nodded his head and said it wasn't like he owned me, but we would have to be vigilant of our schedules. I told him I thought that was a realistic expectation. We agreed that I would move into the house the following weekend, after I got all my affairs in order.

Of course, there were no "affairs" to get in order. I would just need to pack up my clothes, stash some devices and acquire a couple of burner phones. I still had a phone that was capable of high-level encryption and was impossible to tap or trace. I decided I would stash that one in a hidden compartment in my truck.

I also needed to have some surveillance equipment that I could plant in various locations. I needed to know what was going on and when things were happening. These were devices from my special ops' days, and they were still state-of-the-art.

Nothing Arturo or his men would have could uncover or track these devices.

Chapter Seventeen – Getting Ready To Live With The Devil

I drove back to my parking space and noted that I was not followed at this point. Nevertheless, I parked my truck in my underground spot and climbed into my leathers. I contacted Colin, who was working at home. I took off out the back door on my H2R and rumbled easily through the streets. No need to speed or draw attention to myself, I followed every traffic law. If I did have to avoid anyone it could be done very easily on this machine.

I rolled into Colin's driveway and the door opened for me. I pulled in next to his car, got off my bike and removed my helmet and leathers. Colin said that I had clearly had quite an adventurous week. I smiled and told him our plan was coming together and I was moving closer to the inner circle.

We went straight to his situation room and sat in the chairs to discuss what was going to happen next. I described the house and the connected staff house and other details for him. We constructed a floor plan of each location ensuring that access and egress points were all clearly identified. We agreed that, if things went in the gutter, we must at the least have an understanding of what was where.

We also talked about me needing to have my own water hidden as well as some type of protein bars and other food.

You never know what these people are capable of, and preparation was always key to success. I also had some poison reversal drugs that were fact-acting and had already saved my life once during active duty. Preparation is what had kept me alive during my service and out of any serious trouble since.

Colin had also joined my new gym and had been training there for quite a while. We did not connect there; we did not chat or socialize. To all outward appearances, we were simply two people who trained at the same gym. That gym was always busy and there were people everywhere, so it was easy to disappear in the crowd.

I dressed very conservatively, keeping my usual workout gear covered by a loose shirt and loose pants. I did not want to stand out, I wanted to appear like just another woman trying to shed a few pounds. I even toned down my power workouts to avoid any spotlight. We decided that the gym would be the best place to alert one another that we needed to talk. We would not talk at the gym; we simply established a way to notify the other that a discussion was required. Once we did, we could either meet somewhere safe, go to Colin's house, or simply speak on the phone.

I felt like we were in synch, and we began to talk about the plan. We talked about my next steps, our goals and what our end game was.

We both knew that the end goal was to get me as close to El Rey as I could get. We knew it would take time to do that and it would not be easy. At this point it looked to be as long as a one-year operation. I was ready, and I knew what we had to accomplish. There was some trepidation on both our parts, but I knew we were moving ahead.

My next step would be to identify what I would next do to ingratiate myself to Arturo and start my climb up the organization. It was the most dangerous of strategies, I would always need to be on my game .

These guys were typically not at the top of the IQ scale, but they made up for their lack of intelligence in other ways. They were always ruthless, slow to trust, and suspicious of just about everything. That was how they stayed alive and how they advanced their lawless ventures. They may not have been geniuses, but they were all most definitely street-smart in the most dangerous of ways.

My defence was to use my training, intelligence and understanding of their psyche against them. I KNEW how they thought and felt. I KNEW what scared them the most and I KNEW their weak spots. That was why taking the security angle was the simplest and best method to infiltrate the organization. Using my electronic devices to help identify exact weaknesses and areas to prey upon was my ace in the hole.

I knew for certain that every room in that safe house would be bugged. I knew there were cameras there as well. That was an easy decision, given what I had seen in the main house. I could use those to advance my own cause too, letting them hear only what I wanted them to hear.

We finished up, set our contact cues in place and I went to grab some clothing and the electronic gear I needed. I went back to Colin's and set up my surveillance equipment for him in the situation room. He would now have access to all the internet traffic, including messages, coming to, and leaving from that house.

We hugged as I left and drove South to my new "home." I went back to my parking spot, locked up my bike and gear and fired up my truck.

I was buzzed through the gate when I arrived and parked on the side, away from the main house in a row of other vehicles. One of the men showed me inside, carrying one of my bags for me. We dropped everything in my room and then sat at the kitchen table where he described my place and what my main concerns were.

He placed a couple of P226's on the table and said they were mine. I pushed them back to him and said that I preferred my own, I didn't like the 9 mm Sig. I said I found them noisy and too destructive. He asked in a demeaning tone what my preferred pistol was then.

I said the Beretta Tomcat was my close-range weapon of choice. Although chambered in only a .32 calibre, it was quick, palm sized and virtually never jammed. One could hide them anywhere, they had enough stopping power, and they were much quieter than a nine mil. For me, they were really a weapon of last resort anyway as I typically did not require a weapon to gain the upper hand.

I got up, told him I was going to unpack, and went to my room. I closed and locked the door behind me and began to put some things away while I surveyed the room. As I unpacked, filled the drawers, and hung some things in the closet, I closely scrutinized the room. There was a clock on the wall which I suspected held a camera. It was in the perfect spot to get a complete, wide-angle view of the living quarters.

There were a few places where listening devices would be placed, so I simply assumed they were there. I had already decided that if I did have a conversation in that room, it would be with the knowledge that it WAS being listened to by someone. I could plant whatever I wanted them to hear. I would need to observe closely, monitor what I could, and utilize that information to create the tactics required to execute our strategy.

Due to the way these organizations worked; I knew that an opportunity would eventually present itself.

It might be Arturo's mistrust of an underling or partner. It might even be the conduit between Arturo and El Rey, and I knew there would be more than one of them. It would remain to be seen which would present the best opportunity.

I settled in, had a snack, and prepared to sit with Arturo and the man that seemed to be his "top guy." The fellow I was speaking to knocked on my door and said Arturo was waiting for me out by the pool. I pulled on some shorts and a T shirt and headed out there. The pool area really blew me away as I took it all in once again. I could easily see how people could get used to this, especially those who came from poor backgrounds. I wondered how many of these guys had started out on a gravel driveway in tattered jeans.

Arturo pointed me to a chair and his man sat on his left, both of them across from me. His name was Javier, not unusual based on his appearance. He was tall, dark haired and thickly muscled. Clearly of Hispanic descent, he had almost movie-star good looks to go with his obvious power and strength.

Javier was a stark contrast to his own sidekick who had a pockmarked face and was nowhere near as ripped. He did appear to have an edge to him though and I knew he too could be dangerous.

I expected that fellow was likely a knife man, a razor-sharp blade his favorite weapon. As he reclined in a lounge chair close by, I could see the outline of a scabbard on one leg. Guys that looked like him always had knives, usually big knives. Making up for other shortcomings I figured.

Arturo said that Javier was his most trusted associate. He explained that Javier would, without hesitation, put himself in harm's way to save Arturo. That was the loyalty he expected of all his people. If they could not commit to that they could not enjoy the benefits of working for him. He went into some detail about the benefits that included boats, cash, and women. I just smiled and interjected that I was good with the cash, the other two were of little interest to me. He laughed and said I had not yet seen his boat; I may want to reserve judgement.

That was where that part of my day almost ended. Javier and his sidekick were dismissed. Arturo then gave me a wad of cash and told me to do some shopping. He wanted me to appear as if I was legal counsel. Although I would never be portrayed as such, it was the look that he wanted. He felt it safest if I was underestimated by his enemies and those around him. Only he and Javier were left in the organization who were witnesses to my annihilation of his two men in the cage.

I was the definition of a sleeper.

Even though Arturo had only seen a portion of my skills he had tagged me as the secret weapon. He said I was the 800 HP hot rod amongst a whole bunch of street cars. I chuckled inside that he had no idea that what he really had was a jet fighter amongst those street cars. I was confident that we would succeed. I only hoped that law enforcement did not somehow get involved as I would be viewed as nothing more than a criminal. That was the second, very real, danger of operating the way we were. Colin would be unable to protect me, and neither could Norie. I was on my own and as far as any legal people were concerned, I too was a criminal.

I thought how ironic it would be if I got busted while doing this but never caught for all the murders I had committed. I knew killing Bobby and the others was behind me. It was what they call a cold case these days. There are all kinds of TV shows now that show cold cases being solved every day. In fact, that is simply not what happens. Most simply die a slow death in dust-covered, cardboard boxes ignored on long rows of shelves.

Unless I made a critical error, like the Golden State Killer did, I was confident I would never be caught. However, it wasn't only his error that got him caught. The police searched genealogy websites and got a familial match to former police officer De Angelo.

From there, it was a simple case of connect the dots as they worked through the family trees. Once they had a list, which DeAngelo was on, they simply had to get his DNA. They did and shortly after, a forty-year-old crime spree, which involved a dozen murders and over fifty rapes, was solved. I knew that I had left absolutely zero DNA anywhere. There was no chance I could get caught the same way. I was educated, trained, and indoctrinated to leave no trace during my operations.

I wanted to speak with Colin about putting in a solid backstory. We could start by him saying he was working on this case. We could also say that I was acting as his agent. Thanks to his new position at the bureau, he would be able to conduct this type of operation in relative secrecy. He could read in his direct boss with the proviso that, due to the reach of the cartels, he needed to act independently.

A setup like that might protect me should I ever be arrested while connected to this organization. There was no guarantee it would, but I could discuss it with Colin the next time we had the opportunity to communicate. I would like to know I had some sort of backstop to keep me out of prison for the rest of my life should something happen.

I was still doing good work and continuing to rid the world of criminals, but law enforcement and judges did not care much for vigilantes. For them everyone, even the worst scum on the earth, deserved due process.

I did not completely agree with that concept!

Chapter Eighteen – The Daily Drudgery Of Being A Criminal

Much as I despised shopping, I shopped diligently to build the look that Arturo wanted. It was far more difficult than I expected. They simply do not design or manufacture the type of dressy clothes that fit someone like me. This has always been a bit of a curse. Don't get me wrong, I much prefer to be me rather than some size four or size six Barbie, but it would be nice to have more clothing options.

I don't favor dresses or skirts. I found that it was a challenge, with my butt, to get something that fit me well. I ended up having a terrible day and decided I would have to keep looking. That was when the military occurred to me. I recall seeing female officers in dress uniforms that seemed to fit perfectly. So, there WAS clothing that would fit me, I just had to find it. Eventually, on this day, I went back almost empty handed.

I saw Javier and I explained my problem to him. He said they had a tailor who designed and sewed their suits for them. He explained they were constructed to fit perfectly and also allow them room to hide weapons. He said he would check with Arturo, but he felt there would be no problem to hook me up. That was easy. It appeared that Javier would be the go-to guy for all this type of detail.

The next day, after a run, Javier and I sat outside to review schedules, floor plans and other critical details I needed to know. We went over the challenges and benefits of this location, what to watch for and where the safe spots were. He provided all the detail I would need and, unknowingly, gave me some excellent spots to plant listening devices and miniature cameras. I would even use Arturo's own network to broadcast!

When we were done, he said that he had contacted the tailor and he would be over this afternoon. I was a little anxious but happy that I was going to get this handled. I went to my room for a shower, wondering if there was even a camera in here that I had not yet found. I knew for certain there was a listening device as the place was covered with them.

After lunch I was summoned back to the safe house. We were all equipped with tiny, ear bud communicators that were invisible to the naked eye. They were buried deep inside the ear canal and so small that nobody could see them or the miniscule antenna. I recognized Javier's voice telling me my appointment was here and was waiting in the house.

I walked inside to find a tall, younger Asian man with a tape measure around his neck. He was not what I expected, other than the Asian part. He looked more like an actor or a model, to be honest. He extended his hand, and I shook it and introduced myself.

He said he had been dressing the guys here for quite a while, but this was the first time he had to dress a woman.

I told him that I needed to look like a lawyer, and I did not want to stand out. I wanted to be able to just be there and hopefully not attract too much attention. He asked which weapons I preferred to carry, and I told him about the Tomcats. He knew his pistols, because he immediately commented that you could hide those anywhere, that would be no problem. He went on to tell me that he had developed a paper-thin lead lining that he could sew into pockets to disguise the fact a gun was hidden inside. To scanners and X-ray machines it appeared just like the surrounding fabric. That was some serious technology, and I was surprised that it could be acquired outside operations like the CIA and FBI.

I explained to him, as he took measurements, that I preferred a suit jacket with pants and described the military uniforms. I told him that I would probably need a couple of dresses as well, just in case. Nothing too revealing or restricting. He said that the fabrics he used always had stretch to them just in case something happened that required quick movements.

It took him a while to measure me, and he was writing furiously as he did so. It appeared he was in a design-build mode as he sized me up, adding his ideas at the same time. Now, I was interested to see what he might put together for me.

He left after he was done and said I would have to live with what I had because he could not get back to me for at least a week. I said that was no problem.

The week passed uneventfully, and the tailor finally returned. We went to my room with all the bags he was carrying, and I tried on the first suit. It did feel good. I had never had anything tailor-made for me before. I pulled on the pants, added the shirt and then the jacket. I felt like I wasn't wearing anything it fit so well. I stepped out and he said I looked perfect, what did I think? I felt good. There was stretch in everything and almost no restriction to movement as he had mentioned. He showed me the two gun pockets explaining they were built into every jacket.

I tried on each piece and slowly was increasingly impressed with his skill. As far as I was concerned this guy was a genius, based on my prior clothes-buying challenges. I thanked him and hung everything up in the closet. I left each one in a set with the suit, shirt and whatever else went with it. I did not want to have to think about getting dressed.

I brought all my own training gear with me along with a selection of shorts, tops and running shoes. We seemed to have a lot of spare time on our hands sequestered away in this compound, so I got to train often. That was fine by me, except the lack of sparring partners was a challenge.

You had to have a good sparring partner to stay as sharp as possible in hand-to-hand.

The next day was time for my first trip to the gym from this house. I went to take my truck and Javier suggested I try one of the cars. He pointed out four were for our use, they were 100% legitimate and fully registered to Arturo's "company".

His brilliant cover was a charity organization that helped to build schools in Mexico and provide scholarships to immigrants in the San Diego area.

I suppose looking like a real philanthropist was an advantage when you were trying to cover up being a drug dealer.

I had removed all my devices and anything that could incriminate me from my truck. I knew they were likely going to go over it with a fine-tooth comb, so I was prepared. I was more a motorcycle enthusiast than a car girl, but I admit when I saw the Shelby GT 500, I knew I had to take it out.

It was like me, a bit of a sleeper. The grey colour and no stripes might help it hide but it reeked of power and looked fast even while it was parked. There was no special badging or anything, it looked like a stock Mustang, but it was extremely far from stock.

Javier smiled, said nice choice, and popped the hood. It was a V8 with a supercharger on it. I expected it was in the range of 900 HP. Javier said it was designed and modified to handle the power but even with the beefed-up suspension, steering enhancements and ride controls it was a handful and I needed to be very careful. He smiled as he tossed me the keys and told me to bring it back in one piece. Yeah sure, as I hopped in and turned the key bringing that huge motor to life. Of course, my H2R would demolish this thing in a race but there was no need to share that tidbit with him. I needed my motorcycle life to be totally separate and hidden so I could maintain some semblance of freedom.

I backed out slowly and then idled up the driveway. The gates swung open, and I went down the block to the connector. A couple of minutes and I was on the freeway on ramp. I hit the accelerator and, even after seeing what was under the hood, was surprised by the instant power. I was coming out the end of the ramp into traffic, already at close to 100 mph and had to hit the brakes to avoid a collision.

Wow, the acceleration had driven me back into the seat like I was in a rocket. They had clearly done a LOT of work to this car to ensure it could handle the power and avoid pursuit from just about anything. I calmed down and got to the gym in no time, grabbing my bag off the rear seat, as I got out. I was ready for a good workout and got into it right away.

I was only about five minutes in when I spotted Colin and gave him the signal that I could meet at his house. He acknowledged and we both got back to our workouts. He left about a half hour before me. I finished off with some super heavy lifting and then hit the showers. I scanned the gym as I walked out. I felt certain the car they gave me was lojacked, so they would know where I was, explaining why there was nobody following me.

I left the mustang in the parking lot and walked up the alley to a private garage that Colin had rented. Inside we kept a nondescript car that I could use for these meetings when I could not get to my condo and motorcycle.

I tossed my bag in the back of the run-of-the-mill four year old Honda civic, grabbed the keys from under the seat, and drove off. I was at Colin's in less than fifteen minutes so I felt we could take at least a half hour discussing what had happened so far before I would have to leave and go back and get the Mustang.We talked about the structure that I had seen and who was who. Colin laid out some of the messaging he had seen that was pertinent to our operation. There was no mention of me, which was good. Why would a guy like Arturo, who was higher up than we originally thought, say anything about a new bodyguard? If he would have said something that would have concerned me.

Colin and I worked through a few scenarios and set up additional ways to signal each other. He now had a complete understanding of where I was, how I could be reached, and the general outline of our plan. It had already morphed into a different one as soon as I discovered Arturo was more than just a street dealer. I figured the Arlo relationship was just because they had known each other forever.

It was now clear to me that Arturo from La Jolla was an upper mid-level guy in this organization. Based, on the comings and goings I had seen in only the last three days, he was a much bigger fish than I originally thought. I was already in a trusted position with him, so I knew that I would have to do something to catch the eye of the next guy up. I had to do so without causing Arturo to have any second thoughts or concerns about me though as that would surely get me killed. It was going to be a bit of a tightrope walk to figure out my best next move.

As I drove back South on I-5 I ran through things in my head. I needed to do something that would further ingratiate me to Arturo, without causing too many waves. If someone like Javier sensed there was anything off, I could get myself into trouble from which even I might not escape. These guys were all so jittery about almost everything.

I was amazed there weren't guns going off all over the place, all the time.

I almost missed the off ramp but safely exited the freeway and rolled down the street slowly. I got to the gate, punched in that day's code, and drove around back to park.

Javier was strolling my direction as I got out of the car. He smiled and asked how I liked the ride. I slapped his hand and said it was simply great. All around good day. Nice drive, great workout, it was all good.

I decided I needed to get closer to Javier. He had been a trusted second-in-command for a long while. If I could somehow get him out of the way I believed there was a good chance I may be able to step into that slot. Doing so would enable me to get one step closer to El Rey. The trick was to design the right plan.

A simple drug theft would never work, he was too reliable to do anything so stupid. What was more likely, because it happened often amongst these cartels, would be his defection or cooperation with a different group. Even though these clowns made sick amounts of cash and lived luxurious lifestyles they always wanted more. The obvious play would be for him to take out Arturo somehow and then assume the relationship with the next higher contact. There was always danger in it being too obvious because, as skittish as these guys were, their first thoughts always go to a conspiracy of some sort.

I decided I needed to distract myself and slow my mind a bit, so I went to the safe house to watch a little tube. I figured I would sit out in the shared area as that was where everyone hung anyway. Ideally, it would be just myself and Javier but if there were others that would work too. I walked through the door and there were already three of them watching the Kavanaugh hearing.

Dr. Blasey-Ford was speaking and, before they noticed me, one of the lower-level dudes made a crack that, "he should have just done her right the first time and then ditched the body." I walked over and sat on the couch and said, "now boys, that's no way to talk about a woman." The clown on my left said that no woman could stop him from taking what he wanted. I laughed at him and said that I could, and I wouldn't even break a sweat doing it.

Javier had walked in just then and told the guy to shut up. I was surprised when he made another crack. I caught Javier's eye and he nodded a subtle yes in my direction. That was when I blew loud-mouth's nose up with a perfectly placed backhand. He was screaming and there was blood everywhere as he stood and tried to take a swing at me. I wasn't about to kill any more of these bozos, so

I secured his arm and took him down to an arm-bar, Ronda Rousey style.

I had him pinned and locked down and continued to put pressure on the arm. I knew if I went much further that he would be in a cast for an awfully long time, so I yelled at him to apologize. He yelled out another obscenity at me and I increased the pressure just a bit. He screamed out, "let go, let go. I'm sorry, I'm sorry." I let him up and said that we should finish watching this, it was good to know what was happening in politics.

I knew, after my display, I wouldn't have to put up with any more stupid comments. Everyone settled back in, and Javier joined us, sitting in his chair. It was quite odd watching Dr. Ford describe her sexual attack in detail sitting with four macho-man killers, who obviously had no respect for women. I was certain each had, at one time or another, taken something they wanted without regard for what the woman wanted.

I controlled my rage well and just sat there. Each of us making the odd comment and wondering if this was all true. The wrinkled old senators grilling her looked like those two old guys on the Muppets to me. Funny, odd-looking caricatures of real people. THESE guys are the best our country has to offer? I love America and democracy, but sometimes it is difficult to see the clowns that we put in charge in action. At least that was a common sentiment, not that I thought any one of these guys were able to vote in this country anyway.

We got through that, and we were all still sitting there when Kavanaugh came on. He was loaded for bear; I can tell you that. I got the sense it was sort of like when you thought you were perhaps going to lose an argument.

Just be louder and more brash than anyone else, even if you knew you were wrong.

I will confess, at first, I thought he looked a little too choirboy to have done this but then again it was years ago in high school. That was a different time and a different life for almost everyone I know, myself included.

With very few exceptions, I don't think anyone would pass serious scrutiny of that time in their life. Think back to some of the crap you did in high school? I am not saying I am okay with whatever happened, but it was 35 years ago for him.

The age of these guys, it was standard operating procedure to grab an ass or a breast whenever you wanted. Many did much more than that and it was never discussed. We were all just kids, doing what kids did as far as we knew. For the girls I knew it didn't seem to be a huge issue and short of a physical attack, some even figured that any attention was good attention.

I recalled my first situation like that, when I was young, as we watched Kavanaugh alternate between yelling and almost crying.

It was seventh grade, and we were all at a house party. The parents were upstairs, and all our parents had spoken with them. The usual precautions had been taken. We were all just having fun and listening to music. There were a few couples trying to dance and looking awkward doing it.

At our age, dancing was nothing more than an excuse to hug and grind a little. The boys always grinding a little more than most of us girls wanted and many of us just putting up with it. I remember standing there with one of my friends when this guy came and stood in front of me. I think he was an eighth grader as the girl hosting the party had an older brother a grade ahead of us. I can recall it as clear as if it happened yesterday as I run through what occurred in my head.

Out of nowhere, he smiles, reaches out and puts both his hands on my breasts. He kind of squeezed them, what there was and just smiled at me.

He turns to his buddy and says, "they DO feel good." Just as the word "good" came out of his mouth I moved closer to him. Nobody at my school knew that my brothers had been training me for five years at least, to fend off attackers. He thought he was in, right up until my knee connected hard with his nuts and he went down in a heap.

He was crying and yelling and rolling on the floor when the host's parents came down the stairs. When they asked what happened the only thing anyone said was that I had kneed him in the groin. Nobody, not even the girls, mentioned that he had grabbed me first.

I remain shocked to this day that the parents took ME upstairs, called my parents and had them come get me because I was a "trouble-maker." I even got grounded. I talked to my brothers the next day and they said they were glad that I had learned so well. To add insult to injury, this boy then went around school saying that I stuffed my bra. It wasn't the actual comments that made me so mad, it was that he was the one that started this. I was the butt of many jokes for a long while.

Thanks to my family, the talk at school had negligible effect on me. I knew what happened and I knew that my bra was filled solely by me. When I told my brothers about it, they said they would fix it. I told them not to bother and to stay out of it, I could handle myself. There was no FBI to call in and nobody else who really cared about the truth. I had to rely on my own instincts.

I smiled as I recalled how I cornered him one day away from school. I explained that he had two choices. He could apologize to a few groups of other kids, or I would wait until there were a whole lot of people around and then I would pick a fight with him.

He looked in my eyes and realized that I was serious and already had an inkling I could kick his ass. That was my first bona fide experience that the threat of violence could be much more effective than the actual violence.

I tuned back into the conversation as the guys got louder and louder about what a liar this Kavanaugh guy was. They could see it in his eyes and tell it in his voice. While only one had any post-secondary education they all knew how much drinking went on around that age. Everyone knew.

I told them that he seemed believable but then so was Dr. Ford. It was going to be a tough call, but I predicted the votes would end up along party lines. They were no different than the various drug cartels operating in Mexico and the USA. Things got quieter when I made that comment and Javier caught my eye, giving me a look to dial it back. I felt it was in my best interest at this point to stay closely aligned with Javier. He was the one who was basically my boss, but I also realized a time may come when I would need him to save my life.

In the position I was in I didn't have to take an official outside security watch or even monitor the cameras. I was to be with Javier and Arturo whenever they were off the compound or there were "guests" coming to visit Arturo in the compound. Javier shut the TV off when the guys went outside and then said that he needed to show me the boat.

I was a little leery, and on edge, but hoped this was standard stuff. We went to the nearby marina where there appeared to be around seventy boats of various sizes.

On the drive and during the walk Javier said that we would have times where we would need to be on the boat. Sometimes Arturo would be with us and sometimes not. He said the boat had lots of "safety features" that he would explain. I soon discovered these features were about the safety and secrecy of drugs, weapons not so much, people. I tried to pick out which boat was his, but I was way off.

I was expecting one of those superfast offshore boats but realized that was unlikely at Arturo's level. I nearly broke down laughing when I saw the name on the back of a large sailing craft. In fancy script writing it said Arturo La Jolla across the back. Javier said there was absolutely no sense in trying to hide so why bother trying? He punched in a code on the side of the dark blue hull and a set of steps came out electronically, landing on the dock.

I am not really a boat person, but this thing was impressive. The shiny, dark blue hull looked menacing. I figured it was around 100 or 130 feet long but couldn't be sure. I really couldn't tell because it was so sleek, curving hull and glass everywhere.

Javier explained it was one of the smaller boats in the Superyacht sailing class, but it was also one of the fastest. He explained that rich guys liked to race these things. Arturo, like his boss just loved boats it turned out.

It had a large mast in the centre and then a rigid connection from the top of that mast to the front. Javier said that was where the second sail sits. The larger mainsail rolled into a carbon-fibre compartment projecting from the mast toward the rear of the boat. If I had any doubts that crime paid, and paid well, this little tour helped dispel those thoughts. It was all carbon-fibre and gleaming, brushed stainless steel. I had seen yachts like this but never been on one. I was shocked at the opulence as we began our tour.

There were crew quarters up front for five that also housed what looked like a commercial kitchen to me. We went back up to the deck before we could descend into the staterooms. Javier showed me my small room, with his next door and said there were two more like this. The level of security depended on where Arturo was going and what he was doing.

The craft never left the dock without at least three of the security team, even if Arturo was not aboard.

He showed me the bathroom that the security people used. Granite counters, dual sinks, and a walk-in shower nicer than any I had seen. This thing was amazing.

Through this area was the only obvious access to Arturo's stateroom. There was a lockable bulkhead cutting us off. He took me in to show me Arturo's stateroom and then pointed out there was a second secret exit in case there was trouble. It was disguised in a closet and allowed Arturo to get out quickly without being noticed. Making up names and putting secret doors inside closets, original bunch!

From that exit he could access a tiny two-man submarine, diving gear for two people or the small, but amazingly fast, tender that was stored below. Javier continued the tour by showing me the various storage and secret storage areas on the craft. He said that the secret ones could all be controlled either from Arturo's stateroom, the kitchen area, or the top deck.

Each one was a weighted pod with a tracker on it. If there was any possibility of being boarded, or if law enforcement showed up, the pods could easily be jettisoned. Each pod was equipped with a small electric motor and propeller that would shoot it away from the boat.

Once on the bottom, they appeared on sonar, or even cameras, to be nothing more than rocks on the ocean floor. They could then easily be retrieved when the threat was dispatched.

We finished the tour and drove back to the compound where we discussed the next day's schedule. For the most part Javier and I would stay close to Arturo on the compound except for late in the day when he had an off-site meeting. He said that we would be taking the Escalade just to be safe.

I would pose as the driver and Javier and Arturo would sit in the rear. He said there were some tricks to driving it as it was much heavier than your typical escalade. Javier explained it was, for the most part, bullet, and bomb proof. When it was built, they even demonstrated its ability to withstand an RPG hit and keep right on driving. He said that he and I would take it out on a dry run, so I could get comfortable with the handling and performance.

An hour later we got in the vehicle and before going anywhere, Javier showed me how it was equipped. Turns out this thing was your basic James Bond special. It was like those old Aston-Martin's that he used to drive. It even had some of the same extra goodies and a switch that released an oil slick out the rear of the vehicle. There was also a coil of razor wire that could be deployed that would destroy anything following us.

He tossed me the keys after our little walk around and we drove slowly out of the compound. Javier wanted me to drive around on the Pacific Coast Highway and side streets before hitting any freeways so that was what we did. It felt heavier but handled surprisingly well for a vehicle that was likely close to twice the stock weight.

As we rolled up onto the first freeway ramp and I hit the gas, I was a little heavier footed than what was required. I backed off quickly and kept it at the posted speed. I remarked about the power and Javier said that two turbochargers on a larger displacement motor and a custom ten-speed transmission got you that kind of performance.

The ride ended uneventfully and after about three hours we were pulling back into the compound. I felt comfortable with the vehicle and was not concerned at all that I could handle driving it.

I would have liked some downtime to check on the internet traffic and maybe even catch a little nap but there was no opportunity. I supposed it was also good to continue to gather intel too so that was what I prepared to do.

As we went to our rooms Javier said it was a black-tie affair. He said that meant I was to wear one of my suits and ensure that I was packing, including extra clips.

I was extra glad my favorite pistol was the tiny Tomcat. Not only were they smaller and lighter than something like a 9 mm, but the ammo was also about half the weight.

I got changed and Javier was waiting in the group TV room when I emerged. He said that there was no expectation of any trouble, but we always needed to assume there could be trouble.

You never knew what might happen, especially with the current state of the cartels. He said there were power struggles everywhere and Arturo wasn't about to lose any of his turf.

Chapter Nineteen – Cartels 101

I told Javier I didn't know much about these cartels, and he went into great detail for me. He explained about all the cartels and what had happened since El Chapo went away. He said that when a group as powerful and successful as the Sinaloa cartel gets hit like that everyone else wants to step into the void. With an estimated $20 billion US at stake, everyone takes every opportunity to increase their piece of the pie.

He went on to explain that due to deep-seated distrust there was very little chance the cartels would ever cooperate the way the Mafia did in the fifties. I knew that the acknowledged start of these cartels was in 1980 from a fellow who was a former Mexican federal police agent, Miguel Angel Felix Gallardo. Of course, known as The Godfather. From there, many cartels grew, most based on loosely identified geography. The original view was there was enough to keep everyone happy. That feeling did not last long.

I also knew that since the Mexican government declared its war on drugs that many deaths had occurred, on all sides of the conflict. In 2011, when I was deployed there, it was known that more than 12,000 people had been killed in drug related violence in the city of Juarez alone!

The current President of Mexico, Enrique Pena Nieto, who leaves office in December of 2018, continued the fight his predecessor began. Previous President Felipe Calderon was the one who originally decided enough was enough. Calderon had some big Cojones; I can say that with certainty!

When he decided to start this war on drugs, he deployed more than 20,000 soldiers and federal police across Mexico. Four months later, he fired more than 280 federal police commanders as he knew corruption was rampant and that enabled these cartels to be successful.

2008 saw the demise, at the hands of the cartels, of senior Mexican officials. The killing of Mexico's director of investigation for organized crime, the federal police chief and the commander of Mexico City's investigative police force was all in response to the arrest of Alfredo Leyva of the Beltran Leyva cartel in January of that year. That was one time the cartels cooperated, realizing if they did not work together, they could all end up like Alfredo.

The government kept up their war and, although distressed at the loss of life amongst regular citizens, frequently announced their victories in their war on drugs. The brazen attitude of these cartels was on clear display in 2016.

After escaping from prison in 2001 and being captured again in 2014, El Chapo had the audacity to meet with actor Sean Penn for an interview in 2015.

Penn interviewed him, and the article was published in the rolling stone magazine. There is even a series on Netflix called El Chapo telling the story of his beginnings in the Guadalajara cartel and his rise to infamy.

He had escaped through a mile-long tunnel in July of 2015 and met with Penn before he was recaptured by Mexican security forces in Sinaloa. Guzman (El Chapo) was turned over to US authorities in early 2017.

The war continues to be waged with various opinions of its effectiveness. The estimated drug business in the USA connected to Mexican cartels is $20 to $29 billion per year.

I really had little interest in that whole war and all the other cartels. My only interest was in exacting revenge for my good friend Colin. The people I would have to kill along the way did not matter to me. They were simply obstacles in my pursuit of El Rey. My singular goal being to move him from being known as El Rey Do Los Muertos (King OF The Dead) to El Rey que esta muerto (El Rey Who IS dead). I was not in a war on drugs, I was avenging the murder of my friend because of drugs.

Javier knew most of what I did, but it wasn't until we were getting ready to leave that he confirmed what I already knew. He said that our loyalty was to the Mochismo group. Arturo had known them his whole life. He was very highly respected in the organization and if anything were to happen to him it was quite likely all of us would be killed. This was excellent information that I would share with Colin as soon as possible.

It complicated my plan somewhat as this knowledge more or less prevented me from using the current crop of guards, or even Javier as part of my plan. It would be far too dangerous, clearly, to have Arturo killed in the crossfire or chance that the "team" might figure me out.

Now that I knew they were all literally willing to die for him, and to save the others, things were a little different.

We prepared the car and checked all details and then Arturo came out. There were plenty of sentries around the compound, and someone on the cameras at all times, so the compound was always safe. Javier and Arturo got into the rear seats, and I drove us out and towards our destination.

It was an uneventful meeting and I learned little. The meeting was in a darkened room that reeked of tequila. Javier walked in ahead of us and I stayed next to Arturo.

They spoke in Spanish and likely thought, even with my looks, that I could not speak the language. I had let them believe from the beginning I was very much American and could ask where the bathroom was and order drinks but that was about it. In fact, I was fluent in the language as we spoke it in our house all the time and it was one of the few I had learned before and during training.

I watched the men around the table as they spoke of many things. Arturo was animated a few times but they both seemed happy, not agitated. It sounded like this fellow, who I would come to learn was known as El Ruso Negro (The black Russian) had acquired new customers and territory. Apparently, a major geographic competitor of his and his crew had been decimated in car accident. There was nobody to take over, and they had lost seven men, so El Ruso just stepped in and absorbed the business.

The fellow was clearly neither black nor Russian, so I expected his name came from his fierce look. He had a severely pockmarked face and greasy black hair. There appeared to be no visible skin that was not covered by tattoos.

Javier later told me that he killed with pleasure and his nickname was a combination of that and the fact he looked a little like a Russian. They continued speaking as I remained vigilant.

I almost laughed out loud when I heard Arturo quote Sun Tzu to him, "If you wait by the river long enough the bodies of your enemies will float by."

Apparently, Arturo was a fan of the Chinese military strategist, Taoist philosopher and general whose book, The Art of War, is known around the world. Of course, he may just like to gather these little gems from those quote websites too! In this day and age, with internet access and google, you just could never tell.

The meeting went well with both men standing to shake hands. I got a couple of extra looks from El Ruso's men but nothing else out of the ordinary. I was sure they were not used to seeing a woman in my position.

We exited the room and went back to the SUV and drove slowly to the compound. Arturo and Javier had a discussion about what they had seen and how things had gone. Arturo asked Javier if I was learning, and I watched in the mirror as he nodded.

I needed to meet with Colin and discuss what I had uncovered so far and map out a plan.

Chapter Twenty – New Tactics

The next day there wasn't much happening, so I asked Javier if I could take off and have a training day. He said that would not be a problem and I should have a good day. I grabbed my gym bag and rather than use a car, hopped in my truck, and took off. I figured they had likely already planted a tracker somewhere but that was fine. It would show me going to the gym and parked there for a couple of hours. There was no need for deception yet, so I let the tracker transmit accurate data.

It was Tuesday and Colin and I had pre-arranged that he would always be working from home one day each week. Each week the day would advance once. If this week's day were Tuesday, the following week would be Wednesday and so on. It gave us one more option to connect and not display a pattern should we be unable to connect at the gym.

I went through the usual rigamarole just in case I was followed. I drove to the gym, parked my truck, and changed inside. I put on my running gear and went out the back and, when I knew I was not being watched, went down the alley to the garage. Compared to driving that SUV or my hot-rod motorcycle, the four-year-old Civic was a tad boring. Oh well, the life of a spy, I guess. It's not all Aston-Martins and jet aircraft!

I phoned Colin from the burner and let him know I would be there shortly. He had the garage opened when I arrived and closed the door behind me immediately. He said he was glad to see me and asked me how things were going.

I went over all the details with him and took a great deal of time talking about the boat. I said that, at this point, I felt our best strategy might be for me to somehow save Arturo while on his yacht. I told Colin about the speedy little boat, the diving gear and the tiny two-man submarine. I said that I could do this in one of two ways. I would have options depending on how we decided to move forward.

We could contact Norie and give her enough information that, on the next trip, all Arturo's men would be busted. I could escape with Arturo and that would make me top choice. Colin highlighted that it would also position me as the rat unless we used some countermeasures to incriminate one of the others.

The other method would be to again alert a different criminal gang or, better yet, create our own small one with hapless criminals enlisted who would be expendable. We went back and forth many times detailing the pros and cons of each method. Ultimately, we agreed that the safest would be to orchestrate an attempted robbery, like last time, only this time have them succeed.

I could have already planted evidence on one of the other goons. If we were going ahead with this plan, I already decided I would be framing Alonzo, the knife guy. He creeped me out, everything about him screamed deviant criminal. The kind of guy who would do anything to anyone for just about any reason. It wasn't all the tattoos or even his demeanor, it was the ever-present dead look in his eyes. They were always cold and dark, like the depths of the ocean.

Even on a beautiful sunny day, he looked only one day removed from death. I figured I could plant a tracking device on the boat and connect back to anyone other than Javier. We felt that if Javier were gone, I would most likely fill his role and then it could take forever to get to El Rey.

I couldn't wait forever. I needed to get to El Rey alone because I wanted to see the look in his eyes when I explained why I was there. I wanted him to know that my actions were retribution for his order to kill Patti. I wanted to make him experience the same kind of pain that my dead boyfriend had.

With the information I now had access to, and the various devices we were able to track, I could have easily taken a long-range sniper shot. We could accurately predict where El Rey would be and when he would be there. A shot would not be terribly difficult to set up.

Colin would have preferred that, but I was wired a little differently than Colin. I NEEDED this guy to know what he had done had affected many people. I wanted him to know WHY he was being killed.

On one level I contemplated having him experience the same deep sense of loss. We already knew El Rey had a wife and four children, all guarded round-the-clock and living in that fortress. We could take them out but there was a high level of probability that would be a suicide mission. There was also the consideration that, although they were aware what "daddy" did to make money, they were still relatively innocent.

I had to leave soon and get back to the gym as being discovered would likely mean the end of me. Colin and I agreed on the next steps. While I was going about my "job" he was going to purchase a tracking device.

He would do it online, using Alonzo's name. He would have it sent to a post office location that was close to Arturo's mansion have it picked up there and then get it to me. He would search for a guy that resembled Alonzo, according to my description. He could pay him a few bucks to get the package and hopefully show up on a street cam or security camera. The mechanics of getting it done were simple for an FBI guy as experienced as Colin is.

The trail would trace clearly back to our little friend Alonzo. We agreed that I would work out additional details to complete the frame. That was when it hit me. We did not have to literally attempt a robbery and worry about all the logistics and detail that would accompany such a plan. I could simply catch Alonzo after he supposedly planted the device and kill him in a fight.

I would then report back to Javier what happened. There would be subtle clues in Alonzo's room that would lead them to believe that he was indeed tracking the boat for his own reasons. A hidden stash of cash somewhere there would also help assemble the frame.

Once it was established that he was obviously working with someone else I would be even more highly regarded by Arturo. Javier would still be in place, and I could hopefully continue to move closer to El Rey.

Chapter Twenty 1 – Alonzo, The Traitor

It took us a few weeks to get all the details in place. Getting into Alonzo's room to hide evidence against him was not too difficult. I had implanted some simple code in their system that allowed me to blank out cameras. It was not complicated coding or anything. You basically told the camera to take a still photo and then use that photo in a loop. If this occurred for only a few minutes at a time nobody would ever notice anything out of the ordinary.

The next time Colin and I met he gave me the tracking device, the pickup slip for it and a stack of cash. I prepared the slip by burning most of it but leaving a few keys that would lead Javier where I wanted him to go. On the non-burnt sections, you could see the supplier's name, a partial item description and the name Alonzo. I would plant it in Alonzo's trash can.

I planned to stash the stack of cash inside one of the air vents in his room. A slight scraping of the paint on one screw head would lead them to look in there. If not, I would notice it when I was there, which would make me look even better to both Javier and Arturo. I knew that I would need to do everything in one day, so that is what I planned.

I had started to run in the mornings and my path took me past the marina each day. It came up in casual conversation and once Javier was even at the boat and saw me run past. That was perfect, I needed to be sure that my actions were all routine. While I was doing this, I was trying to get a little closer to Alonzo.

I knew that I had to somehow get him to the boat alone so that I could take him out. I had to find a way to build just a little trust, somehow. A couple of times, when we were alone in the TV room, I asked him about some of his tattoos. I recognized the gang ones and did my best to stay away from those. Bringing attention to those would not advance my cause.

He did start to loosen up, sooner than I expected. One day, when we were watching a little tube and Javier was with Arturo, he caught me off guard. The little creep hit on me! I still cannot believe I was able to keep a straight face as I led him on. I had not considered this happening, but it made everything so much simpler. It was humorous that, in their world, a greasy little twerp like Alonzo could feel like he had a chance with me. I am almost three inches taller than him and outweighed him by at least twenty-five pounds.

I am proud to say that twenty-five pounds was pretty much all solid muscle too. Thanks to this little operation, I was training even more than ever.

I had even found a sparring partner at my new gym and that was a tremendous help in keeping me sharp. He was nowhere near my equal, but he was still a good fighter. It is a real advantage to be able to train with someone who has serious skills.

Not that I want to blow my own horn, but Alonzo was a nasty looking little guy. In his head, I was sure he thought he was prettier than Tom Cruise. I was blessed by my genes. My father and mother both being attractive, successful, and physical specimens. I knew I wasn't a mutt and self esteem had never been an issue in my life, although I derived it from my strength and power and not my looks.

I marvelled at how guys like Alonzo viewed themselves when so many women had difficulty appreciating their own good qualities. Many women seemed to see every small thing that they considered a flaw in themselves. It was frustrating to watch. The doubt in the minds of Kathy and Angela got a bit tiring sometimes. Fortunately neither was like that all the time.

But self-esteem was never a problem with these guys. I used that against him and without having to do anything he was now in my web. I just had to find a way to get him to that boat when no one else was close and take him out. Distrust of everything by guys like Javier would do the rest of my work.

I set him up for the next morning. Before he left for his evening guard duty, I told him that he should sneak away and meet me at the boat in the morning. He readily agreed, and the plan was in motion. The dolt figured he was going to get a little action. Ugly and stupid, in this case a deadly combination.

Once he was gone, and I was alone, I triggered the cameras in the main room and his room to go into a loop. I had already prepared the pickup receipt, so I planted that in his small trash can, underneath some other garbage. I removed the grate from the air vent high up in the wall, stashed the cash inside, and scraped up the screw when I closed it up.

I also planted a burner phone that would connect back to him. I was in and out in less than three minutes and I returned the cameras to normal mode.

Morning arrived, and I changed into my running gear and let Javier know I was heading out. I really hoped that Alonzo was not detained, and the situation was good to go when I left for my run.

I ran past the boat and then found a good spot from which to observe. I stretched out behind a tree with a clear view of the deck. I waited for at least fifteen minutes and saw nobody come or go until Alonzo showed up. I was neither worried nor excited, it was just one more step in our plan. I got mentally prepared and then strolled down the dock and boarded the boat.

Alonzo was already in the security crew quarters, so I scanned quickly, making sure it was just us. I was confident that, unless someone was down in the crew area, we were alone.

I went down the stairs and there he was, grinning like a Cheshire cat. I was surprised the idiot wasn't laying on the bed naked surrounded by rose petals. SO dense. He stood up when I entered and came towards me. I held him off and said he misunderstood my intentions. I just wanted to be friends. I knew that would attack his ego and he would most likely get aggressive, which he did.

He came towards me again and tried to grab me and I slapped his hand away and stepped back. "What kind of BS is this Chica?" he said as he again came towards me. I told him I was only trying to make a friend and I wasn't interested in him that way. He reached into the back of his pants, pulled out his knife and said ,"we'll see about that you bitch. Get your clothes off," he yelled out.

I just laughed at him and didn't move at all. This was the first time I saw any kind of emotion in those dark, empty eyes of his. They were lit up with rage, never a good thing in a fight.

I wanted to make this quick, I knew I could easily make it obvious that he attacked me after I disarmed him. Sure enough, he was so blinded, he came at with me with the knife.

He swiped wildly from side to side and on the third swipe I came up under the arm and spun against the swing. I now had a tight grip on his forearm and used my other hand to knock the knife out of his hand. I figured I needed to have a few marks on me, maybe even a small slice on my arm to sell the whole situation. I let him go and stepped away and he came in swinging. I let him connect with a couple of blows to my face before I unleashed a strike that knocked him clear across the small room.

He hit the wall hard, and his head bounced against the stainless-steel wall, further enraging him. He did have the wherewithal to collect his knife off the floor and now he slowly moved forward. He was yapping the whole time about half-breed bitches. I just smiled at him as I waited for the opening, I knew would present itself.

Rather than swing the knife this time he did as I anticipated and tried to stab me. I easily sidestepped his weak attempt and trapped his arm between my own arm and my body. I spun back against him, securing his wrist and the knife, and plunged it deep into his abdomen while it was still in his hand. Now there was a different emotion in his eyes, absolute shock.

Twice in one day, he was really growing as person. Too little, too late, however.

As I twisted, I had crouched lower at the same time, to ensure I could get an upward trajectory for the blade. It entered exactly where I wanted, a couple of inches below his sternum and slipped easily through the flesh. Knife guys always took particularly good care of their favorite weapons, so I knew it would be surgical scalpel sharp.

The full blade was now completely inside his body, up to the bolster. I pushed up harder and twisted, lifting him right off the deck as I did.

His eyes went dead again and that was that the knife shredding his heart, the last bit of life oozing out of him quickly. No more Alonzo.

I left the knife where it was and Alonzo where he fell. I had a couple of bruises and used my own knife to cut my arm to make it look like he had slashed me. I placed the tracking device where I hoped it could be found up on the deck and showered off all his blood from me. I rinsed the blood out of my running gear and put it all in the dryer and calmly waited. Even if someone showed up here now, I would have a story, so I wasn't worried.

Once it was dry, I got back into my running gear and ran back to the house.

I found Javier as quickly as I could and said we had a problem and I needed to speak with him privately. I told Javier that I was on my morning run when I ran past the boat and saw Alonzo hanging over the side. I thought he was in trouble, so I ran down the dock and jumped onto the boat. When I got up on the deck, I obviously startled him, and he asked what I was doing there?

I told him I thought he was in trouble, and I came to help him. That was when I saw something in his hand. I had no idea what it was, but he apparently thought I did. I watched Javier's eyes as I spun my tale, and I could tell the jury was still out for him. I continued, explaining that he pulled his knife on me and forced me down to the security crew quarters. Once we were down there, he asked if I wanted to make even more money, he said he had a plan.

When I said I wasn't interested he came at me with the knife. I explained to Javier I tried to get more information out of Alonzo, but he was hell-bent on killing me, so I had to defend myself. Javier said we needed to go to the boat before anyone else.

We drove down there, and he told me to repeat exactly what happened and not to leave anything out. I went through everything again and then we went down to the cabin area.

He said I had made quite a mess, perhaps I should be the one to clean it. He laughed and told me not to worry, their cleaner would take care of everything, but we would have to tell Arturo first.

We checked his pockets and found nothing and then went up onto the deck. I heard Javier say, "what have we here," and I turned to see him holding the tracker. I was glad he was the one who found it, across the deck and behind one of the winches. He held it up and clearly knew exactly what it was. I knew he would now go through Alonzo's room with a fine-tooth comb and would surely find the cash and the receipt. Things were playing out quite well so far.

We locked up the boat and drove back to the compound. Javier told me to sit at the outside table on the grass and he went to get Arturo. By the time they got to the table Javier had already briefed Arturo, likely giving him a high-level overview. Javier then asked me to tell him the whole story and leave out no details.

I knew this was their way of confirming that I was telling the truth. This was now the third time that Javier would hear my story. I knew I had to alter or leave out some minor details just enough to make everything ring true.

From my extensive interrogation training I knew that if the same story was repeated, with no subtle changes or further recollection, it was most likely not true.

People do not recall traumatic events that easily and in perfect detail. Whether you are talking about eye-witness accounts, or something directly experienced, there were always things that changed.

As the trauma of an incident got further away additional details often surfaced. Your brain works to protect you by blocking certain things but when the adrenalin rush is gone you tend to remember more. It is a proven fact and with these guys being as distrustful and skittish as they were I needed to make sure that I was perfect in the minor imperfections and subtle variations of my story.

By the time I was done they seemed to both be convinced. I apologized for making a mess on the boat. They dismissed me to talk amongst themselves and I walked back to my quarters to change. I was pleased to see there was a guy going through Alonzo's room.

As expected, there was also one going through mine. I went to my door, looked in and told him not to make too much of a mess. That was when he started taking everything out of my room and tossing it all over the bed. I just walked away telling him he would find nothing because there was nothing to find but to have fun looking.

Not too long after that the other guy called him to Alonzo's room. He had found something. I hoped they had the intelligence to have examined the trash can contents closely and also found the money. They left soon after and it appeared they had both "clues." I just laughed on the inside thinking this was like taking candy from a baby. It was so easy to use their own fear, mistrust, and greed against guys like this.

I knew that combination is what would eventually get me to El Rey. I was eagerly anticipating the denouement of this whole operation but needed to ensure that I did not get ahead of myself. You never wanted to look too far past the immediate future. Confusing strategy with tactics could get one killed.

I knew they would find nothing in my room, so I wasn't too concerned when I was called out to the table again. Javier and Arturo were already seated.

As I sat down, I noticed a couple of the other guys not too far away. That got me a little tense, but I was ready for almost anything anyway. Arturo asked me to tell him what happened again. He focussed first on why I was even there. He seemed okay with my explanation of my morning run, especially when it was backed up by Javier.

He then set the tracker down on the table and asked if I knew what it was.

I said it appeared to be a bug or something and asked if that was what Alonzo had with him when I found him? He said it was and wondered if he was acting alone or if I was part of it.

I was ready for the question and chuckled when I asked him if it made sense that I would betray my new family. I said he must be aware that I have no other family or money, so this gig was the best thing to happen to me in years. I get to train all the time; I have lots of money and a very safe place to live. I added that I hoped that after a few years I might get out with all the money I save and live somewhere on an island by myself.

I understood there were risks, but we all live with risks. Our lives seldom go exactly as planned. My meagre military pension did little to help me be happy about my service and I was currently making ten times that amount, tax free too. They both chuckled at that one and things settled down a bit.

Arturo said they had an issue with one of the men about five years ago. Up until now that was the only incident. He went on to explain that, once discovered, he was severely beaten over a few days. As a grand finale he was drawn and quartered, just like in medieval times.

He went into detail, to ensure that I understood that loyalty was everything and without that, death was painful.

Arturo told the whole story as if he was relating tales from a wonderful wedding or happy gathering. He was cold and unfeeling as he described the human entrails as they were ripped from the man's body. He compared it to gutting a fish with the only real difference being the fish was already dead when it happened.

I was a little thrown by not only the story, but the detachment with which he was able to tell it. For the first time, I did not have to fake the disgust mixed with fear that was showing on my face.

After that meeting I knew I had been thoroughly vetted, my room had been completely torn apart and they almost fully trusted me. I also knew that Arturo was happy that I had discovered Alonzo's bug as that could have cost him millions and perhaps even his life. Saving the right life in their world was always a trust-builder. Once they considered their own mortality, they put much more weight on that than mistrust or fear.

Things settled down a bit and slowly got back to normal. One of the other guys even shared that he was glad I had killed that "little creep." He had never trusted Alonzo and we were all better off without him.

He went on to tell me he had seen Alonzo kill many people with his knives. He knew of nobody that was as accurate and deadly as he was.

He was fast, sneaky, and surgical with those weapons. He had watched people who did not even know they were cut fall to the floor and bleed to death in seconds.

He said he was extremely impressed that I could take him out like that and if he was ever in a knife fight, he wanted me with him. I just said likewise and tried to look sincere.

Chapter Twenty 2 – I Need A Break.

I needed some normalcy in my life so I decided to ask Javier if I might have two or three days off. I told him that after the whole Alonzo thing I was really stressed, and it would help me to re-focus if I took a little break. He did not tell me so, but I knew he would check with Arturo first. He came to me the next day and said there was little happening, if I wanted two days, I could leave Friday afternoon and be back bright and early Monday.

I thanked him and said that was great and I really appreciated him letting me do that. He just smiled and said, "this place isn't a prison. In fact, it is designed to keep us all OUT of prison." He told me to return with the focus and commitment he had seen so far and there would be no issues.

I was hoping for a party at Jonathon and Kathy's house as I drove my truck out of the compound and headed up the PCH. You kind of had to get on and off the Coast Highway after leaving La Jolla as, heading North, you ran straight into Camp Pendleton. I knew that, but still wanted to be on that highway as much as I could, so I skipped the freeway.

Whether riding or driving, having that ocean on one side of me was invigorating. I loved the smell of the salt air and the sound of the waves crashing against the shore.

I was truly in heaven when on a motorcycle and I could feel the breeze against my face. I liked the way it cooled the effects of the blazing sun which burned in Southern California all but six weeks of the year, during rainy season.

I still had the H2R and was eager to get on that thing and wind it up on some curvy roads. I drove the truck to where I had the bike parked, grabbed my gear from a locker and suited up. I loved the feeling of invincibility when I put on my leathers. It was loaded with armor plate throughout the jacket and pants and was pretty much the same as the people who raced superbikes wore.

Superbike racers, with their ridiculously expensive and fast machines, raced at over two hundred mph. Thanks to their perfectly designed protective gear those guys often survived crashes, even at those speeds. It wasn't a lot of fun to skid along asphalt at 150 mph or so but what's a little heat and bruising when you at least end up alive? To those guys, a few broken bones and rashes were nothing. They were all aware of the alternative.

I enjoyed the feel of the gear against my body. I felt a little like a super-hero, but I knew that a crash occurring outside of the track had nowhere near as high a survival rate as one that happened on the track.

I always kept things realistic and rode as safely and intelligently as I could. Anticipation was always the best defense when riding out in the real world, just like in the rest of my life.

I phoned Colin before I left and was happy to hear there was a party this weekend. I really did need a break. But first I needed a good rip on the bike to clear my head. I always found that the intense focus required to ride a powerful motorcycle around traffic helped me to calm down. On most people it had the opposite effect but for me it was both liberating and relaxing. It was like an elite hockey player where they say the game slows down for them. Even though they are operating at top speed most of the time, they can see and sense things before others do. The greats in any sport always amazed me because of that.

Some days I wished I would have kept playing hockey, but I never really seemed to fit in. It appeared to be almost an exclusively white girl sport when I was playing, and I didn't quite fit that mold. Besides, I was already far too busy training and working on other sports. I could never make the commitment to hockey and that was quite fine with me.

I let Colin know I would be at his house in a couple of hours and motored on. The feel of the breath-taking power and the precise handling of the bike was euphoric.

I weaved in and out of traffic and when I found stretches of quiet road, I gave the throttle a twist and rocketed ahead. I could have ridden for hours and hours up and down the coast. Running inland to the hills, now and then, where I knew the curvy roads would provide an exhilarating ride. But I had my three hours or so and then rode directly to Colin's house.

He heard me roll up and the garage door opened so I rode straight in. I hopped off my bike as the door closed and started to climb out of my leathers, piling things on the floor around my bike.

Colin gave me a big hug and started peppering me with questions before we even got into the house. I explained to him that I would tell him everything but when the sun came up tomorrow, that was it. No "business" talk until Sunday afternoon.

He understood the pressures and challenges of undercover work, so he readily agreed to my conditions. We sat out on the deck and enjoyed the sunset with a bottle of wine as I laid out for him exactly what had happened. He shared with me what he had found out via our monitoring devices and otherwise, since we last spoke. Not too much it turned out.

He was pleased to tell me the coroner was safe as was his family. There was nothing to indicate that anything was in the works. His job was done, and the report had been prepared as they needed.

There was no need to kill him because there was no evidence he was coerced. The chance of him talking was almost zero. Colin was sure, as far as the crooks were concerned, the coroner was a closed matter.

We talked a little about Arturo's boat and the whole scene with Alonzo. He was happy the plan worked and was eager to get going on the next steps. Of course, it was a very fluid situation, and we would be forced to be reactive, but that didn't mean we couldn't at least hash out a general game plan.

I wanted to discuss with him another concern. As Arlo had been our way in and that was how I first met Arturo I was worried that we might end up in the same place at the same time. I knew we could not share any part of our plan with Arlo or Sage, but I also felt obligated to protect them. I asked Colin if there were any black ops type sites where we might be able to comfortably hold them until this was over? Of course, there were a few but he thought we might have an easier time if spoke to Norie.

In her senior position, and with the ear of Jackie Lacey, Norie had become powerful. She had access to witness protection locations and all kinds of other things of which the public has no knowledge. It was decided we would invite Norie over on Sunday afternoon and read her in on the whole plan.

She was sympathetic to our cause, had participated in illegal activities with me before and knew Patti and Colin well. Norie understood we were going after these guys, and she would do whatever she could to support us.

I trusted Norie with my life at this point.

We polished off the wine and some snacks and I told Colin I really needed to get some sleep. I asked him to just let me sleep as late as I wanted, and he agreed. He showed me to the guest room and then went off to his situation room to add details and facts he had learned from me today. I guessed he would probably spend at least two hours in that room. That was just how he operated.

I crawled into the big, cushy bed and was out in minutes. Thanks to the blackout blinds and a quiet air-conditioned house I did not step out of that bed until close to 11:00 AM. Very uncharacteristic for me, so it was clear I had been absorbing some stress. I felt refreshed and good to go when I went downstairs for my coffee.

We chatted about everything and nothing as we sat there staring out at the Pacific. The water seemed to change so much throughout the day as the sun moved deliberately across the sky.

It wasn't just the tides; it was the colors and the shapes of the waves as the earth rotated slowly around the sun. The moon circling the earth once each 24 hours, its gravitational pull affecting the tides. It truly was mesmerizing and an amazing thing that unfolded every day. I suggested we grab a few waves before the party and Colin was all over that idea. I hadn't surfed since this whole thing started and I really needed a board fix.

We waxed up a couple of boards and got into wet suits and were paddling out in no time. The waves were looking good for this time of day. Set after set rolling in and cascading softly onto the sandy beach. There were a few people out but not as many as one would expect, which was simply fine with me. We paddled out to a favorite spot and then waited. It wasn't long before I was grabbing my board and jumping up quickly to get my feet under me.

And there it was! The sun warming my face as the salty air and cool blue water splashed up. I glided smoothly along the top of my first wave not wanting it to end. I eased down the face and then quickly turned back up only to slide down once more and repeat the whole thing again. I enjoyed absorbing the changes with my legs and core for what seemed like hours on each wave but was surely no more than a minute.

Up and down, I carved turn after turn, experiencing the joy of a shorter more performance-oriented board.

I was sure if the Big Kahuna were alive, he would mock my use of such a toy compared to the nine-, ten-, and twelve-foot behemoths he made famous. When Duke Kahanamoku brought surfing to the masses he surfed a ten-foot board that was larger than most of today's massive stand-up paddleboards. Of course, in Duke's day, surfboards were really BOARDS. Shaped and gracefully curved but solid wood boards, nevertheless. You could easily be killed if one of those hit you on the noggin.

Today's surfboards have evolved over the years. Perfectly shaped foam cores beneath gleaming, baby-butt smooth fibreglass or plastics. The new boards are certainly lighter and much more maneuverable but the feel of one of those old boards was amazing. If you ever rode one you were instantly transported back in time, imagining yourself riding waves with Duke or Gidget. It was similar to the feel of driving a '57 Chev versus one of today's plastic, screaming four-cylinder little boxes.

We stayed out for about two hours and each of us had some great rides. I could have stayed right there all day, but the waves flattened out and soon there were none, just a massive expanse of eerily flat ocean. We paddled in slowly, sad that the riding was over.

We slipped up onto the beach right in front of Colin's house and showered off outside after spraying off the boards and getting them into the racks.

I was now excited to get to the party and see everyone. I was ready to be in a completely safe place, relaxing with real friends and sipping on as many icy coronas as I wanted. We went in and had some light snacks and a beer and then went our separate ways to get ready.

I had left clothes and bathing suits at Colin's before all this started in anticipation of just such a "vacation." I showered, spent the usual 30 seconds doing my hair, and got dressed. I grabbed my favorite shorts and a tank top and was ready to go. As I expected, Colin was wearing some board shorts and a loud Hawaiian shirt, one of those Tommy Bahama ones, I think. I asked him if there was an off switch for that thing and he just laughed and said no way.

His shirt reminded me of the Ocean Pacific clothing that was so popular when I was in school. It seemed like everyone wore OP clothing and most of the guys had a puka shell necklace to go with.

It was a simpler time and one I sometimes missed. Your only worry was your next thrill, and an occasional test. The odd party too of course. I didn't really have to worry about tests, ever. Even in college my comprehension and recall were outstanding.

I did not have an Eidetic memory or anything like that, I just seemed to learn very quickly and retained almost all of it. Luckily for me I could puke it all back up on a test paper whenever I had to.

I think that was how I got tapped by the special forces. I'm sure they had "scouts" at various top-level universities to watch for people like me.

I was an honor student, a three-sport athlete, and in the kind of physical condition they coveted.

It should have been no surprise they had a scout at George Mason University. An odd choice for a California girl, but it was their criminal justice programs and faculty that attracted me. I had to pay almost twice the in-state tuition to attend but it was worth it. The program was known across the states so why wouldn't I expect the CIA, FBI, and others to troll there for recruits?

I was incredibly pleased, when I accepted the offer to go to Special Forces, to discover my $200,000 plus student loans would be forgiven. As soon as I was ready for active duty, the loan would simply disappear.

They had never mentioned that particular "signing bonus" but it was a weight off my shoulders when the balance suddenly showed as zero.

When I looked at the date it was the exact same day that I was deemed ready for active duty.

At least so far, they appeared to be men of their word.

I was still ready to party now that I had done a little reminiscing about my school days.

Chapter Twenty 3 – Party Time

Colin grabbed us each a nice cold Corona and we made the short walk up the beach to Jonathon and Kathy's. The party was already in full swing, but we were spotted as soon as we stepped up off the sand. First Kathy and Angela rushed up to us and then Jonathon and Luke joined the group hug. It really was good to see them all again.

We sat around one of the tables, closest to the beer fridge of course and the chatter started. It was like I had never left. I looked around the table wondering what my friends would think if they knew what I was really doing, what I had done. It didn't matter as they never would know. My life was always a complete separation of church and state and it had to stay that way. Norie and Colin were part of my tiny inner circle, but they were both there for good reasons.

We snacked on appy's and drank various concoctions created by Jonathon as we all talked a mile a minute. Jonathon asked if I was happy with my portfolio. I said of course I was and asked why, was there something I should know. After confirming I had not reviewed anything for a few months he was almost giddy when he told me that things were going very well. He suggested I sign on tomorrow and have a look and then said to himself, "thank you Jonathon, thank you very much."

I watched the people as we talked, caught up with each other's lives and drank. I didn't see Sage or Arlo, which was good, and then spotted Norie. I waved at her and yelled out her name and she came over to our table. Colin pulled in an extra chair between us and Norie took a seat. Jonathon got her a drink and she pretty much downed it, explaining it had been a particularly challenging day. Then she was all over me about where I was, what was going on, how was I? We all chatted for hours until the sun began to set and then Jonathon decided we should all go inside. The party had slimmed down a bit, and it was just our little group.

We went in and played some games and had some more drinks and when I got Norie alone I asked if she could meet us at Colin's tomorrow. I had something we really needed to discuss. She said sure and then we all just continued having fun and acting like fools. Finally, things settled down and we said we were taking off.

We had invited Norie to stay over so I'm sure there was some tongue-wagging when the three of us strolled down the beach to Colin's house.

Nothing nasty, just something I was certain they would tease us about down the road.

I was eager to see what Jonathon has been referring to so when I got into the guest room at Colin's I used the spare computer for a little bit.

After Jonathon's comment the suspense was killing me and I did not want to wait until the morning to find out what he was talking about. I got ready for bed and then switched on the computer.

It took a little while and I was about to just shut it down when the investment site screen finally popped up. I keyed in my username and passcodes and waited for everything to load. I scanned line by line but it's not like I would notice individual changes anyway, so I have no idea why I bother. When I got to the bottom of the second screen, I did notice a change.

I stopped myself from yelling out at the shock of my total portfolio value. I had not checked it in a few months. When I had last been on the site the total value of my investment was a little more than $2.2 million. That was awesome considering it started at $20,000, which Jonathon quickly turned into $600,000. Thanks to his brilliant advice it had climbed to that two million plus amount. But this new number was even more amazing to me.

The grand total on the lower right corner of that screen now indicated I had $4,235,674.00 across all my investment accounts. I was a legitimate millionaire I realized. Not a Jerry Buss millionaire or anything crazy, but still a millionaire! I was ecstatic. Money had never motivated me, and I had been quite fortunate in how things had turned out for me. Still, it was nice to realize I now had NO financial worries.

I couldn't wait to see Jonathon next. I hammered out a quick email to him on my phone thanking him profusely for his efforts and what he had done for me. I added that I hoped everything was legal and above board along with a smiley face.

I knew he would never jeopardize what he and Kathy had so I felt it was something I could joke about.

Chapter Twenty 4 - A New Teammate

The sun seemed to rise extra early the next day. I know that's not possible but the way my head felt it sure seemed like it had. I wandered into the kitchen in search of my morning coffee and was pleased to find it had just finished brewing. Nothing like a hot coffee and Bailey's and sitting in the cool morning, ocean air that was gently wafting in over the Pacific.

Colin had picked up some scones and other breakfast things and we all sat out on the deck and had breakfast. I told Norie that Colin and I had found Arturo. I warned her to stay calm and said that she could leave at any time and then began to lay out what had been going on. I told her everything that had happened up until now and my plan to get past Arturo and get after the real culprit. She was a little shocked at the details.

I knew that a case like this, if it were to be a real case, would vault her to the top. If she were to successfully prosecute these guys, she would be a shoo-in as DA whenever she wanted to run. I also knew, as did she, that such a case would put an even bigger target on her head. We knew these people stopped at nothing to keep their criminal enterprises intact and making them bucketsful of cash. I was pleased when Norie looked at us and said simply, "we should keep this one off the books."

It was a large sacrifice for her and her career. We discussed that and said we could still play it either way. Colin wanted El Rey to suffer and die but that end could be accomplished in prison too. Although it would be much more difficult to orchestrate. Prison actions against such a powerful cartel drug lord were fraught with challenges. We all soon agreed that we would stay the course. We would now have Norie more actively working with us and that was good. It would allow me to stay further ahead of any law enforcement as Colin had the FBI covered and Norie would have both the state and local law well in hand. We were a solid team and had a singular goal. We were ready to take the next steps.

I laid out for Norie that I believed it would be much safer for Arlo and Sage if we were able to sequester them away somewhere. We discussed the connection to Arturo and the fact that Arlo was the one who got me in there. I didn't want to risk any sensitive information accidentally being passed along. It would not end well if Javier, Arturo, or anyone else discovered my friend Colin was an FBI agent and my other friend Norie was a high-flying ADA.

Norie said she did have access to a location, and she could bury it for quite a while within another case. Arlo and Sage would be well taken care of and guarded twenty-four seven. Their cover story would be a trip South, which they often took for an extended period, so nobody would be any the wiser.

We decided that the easiest way to do this would be to contact Arlo and Sage and invite them to a dinner party at Colin's tonight. We all agreed that it would be best if we told them that they needed protection but did not share the details as to why. It would be Colin selling the whole thing, from an FBI perspective, even though it would be Norie's people helping us.

Norie got everything ready with the special detail and told them where they would be picking up the witnesses. These things were often done with little notice so that was not out of the ordinary. She provided the details of the house and let it slip they were doing a favor for the FBI. That was not untrue, as we were indeed helping Colin. Mostly, I did not want to risk the operation or see Sage or Arlo hurt or worse.

They showed for dinner, we laid out the story and they seemed happy to be going on an all expenses covered vacation. I think everything was an adventure for those two. Once Arlo was advised they could bring their stash he was even happier. The detail disappeared with them and none of us knew their location after that.

When the coast became clear Norie had a contact number to call, and they would be returned.

Chapter Twenty 5 – Back To Work

We all finished at Colin's, and it was time for me to get back to work. We had agreed that we would discuss a plan on our next meet once I had a chance to determine if there was any additional fallout from the Alonzo situation.

I reversed my steps and was soon driving leisurely down the PCH towards the compound. I was a bit anxious, usually when I got those feelings it was for a reason. I was not overly concerned but was a little on edge when I rolled through the gates and parked my truck. I was prepared for almost anything as I stepped out and walked towards the house. Javier spotted me and began walking towards me, meeting me by the table.

Javier welcomed me back and asked me to walk with him. He told me they had traced the GPS bug back to Alonzo, but they were still surprised it was him. He went on to say how long he had been with them and the things he had done for them. He shook his head, looked directly into my eyes, and said, "I guess you just never know." I met his gaze and went back at him with, "trust is over-rated in my books. I think almost anyone can be swayed with the right threat or offer."

He said that we would need to be extra vigilant, and I agreed. He told me that we should trust no one and always ensure the best precautions are in place. I smiled inside at his comment as I had no idea how these guys could become any LESS trusting of people, especially those around them.

Rather than advance our plan, as I had hoped, the Alonzo situation may have set it back a bit. Only time would reveal if that were the case or not. Javier said he was glad I decided to come back early as they had a meeting that he would prefer I attend, black tie. I nodded, confirmed the time, and went to my room to prepare.

I got dressed, loaded my Tomcats, and clipped them inside my jacket. I loaded an additional four clips and stashed them as well. For good measure I strapped my Wasp knife to the inside of my calf, concealed in a padded sock.

The Wasp knife was originally designed to protect divers from sharks. When you stab something under water it injects a ball of freezing gas, at 800 psi, into the target. That ball balloons to the size of a basketball immediately and freezes the internal organs. It kills the target while simultaneously sending it to the surface. Once at surface pressure the target explodes. This gives the diver an opportunity to escape the area while the blood is attracting other predators at the surface.

The knife, as one might assume, is also highly effective on land. It can be quite messy however, and one must be prepared for that. I have used it twice and prefer to be behind the victim when I stab them in the chest or stomach. Usually, the body will explode out the front and I can stay clean.

If I was able to choose a weapon, I still preferred the garotte. It was simple, clean and could be hidden in plain sight. It was best used covertly, sneaking up behind the person, so would not work here anyway. I only bought the wasp knife to wear while surfing but then thought it might be quite handy to have in tricky situations, besides shark attacks. I did not often require a knife but when I did that was a good one to have. I got the sense this evening might be a good day to have it.

I was all ready and met up with Javier and one of the boys while we waited for Arturo. Javier said that we needed to be on high alert. This guy was a partner but also a rival. Arturo had been advised by his boss that there might be an issue, so we needed to be prepared.

Arturo was also wearing a suit and he looked a little heavier or something. I would later find out that he often wore a state-of-the-art ballistic vest that protected his major organs. The vest was very thin and, while you would be left with a healthy bruise if you were shot, only armor piercing rounds could penetrate it.

I figured it was a waste of time because if someone were coming after him, he would be taking rounds in the head, not the body.

Javier sat in the back with Arturo and the third man, Bobby, was driving. Javier gave me the address to program into the GPS and we took off. San Diego, like all major cities, has its good neighborhoods and bad ones. Generally, the worst areas carry high crime rates, lower property values, low incomes, and high unemployment. This combination makes for a pressure cooker of drug and gang related activity and violence.

As we drove deeper into San Diego from our beautiful, ocean-view compound this became increasingly apparent. With the other dude driving, I was able to survey everything along the way. As we got closer to our destination you could see drug dealers plying their wares on the steps of old missions and churches. Jittery, long-haired men and rough-looking women buying their daily fix from an equally unkempt and sad individual. Lookouts lounged lazily on each corner to warn him of any police nearby or approaching danger.

Judging by the GPS I knew that our destination was in the Mount Hope neighborhood. Broken down houses, apartments and housing projects made it look as poor as it was. Sure, San Ysidro was purported to be the "worst" neighborhood in San Diego, but I think once you got to this level, they were all about the same.

Mount Hope was filled with anything but hope. It had low house values and a median income below $37,000 per year. The thing that struck me is we were mere miles from neighborhoods where $37,000 was the median MONTHLY income. I knew that right close to those folks lived people for whom that same $37,000 was a weekly income. Yes, it could never be said that California was not a place of sharp contrast. It always had been and always will be. The elites getting richer and richer while the wretched poor cut their grass and take care of their yards and children.

Mount Hope is between the I-15 and 805 freeways with interstate 94 cutting it off at the top and Imperial Avenue on the bottom. The only thing it had going for it was the year-round perfect San Diego weather. We were driving on Market Street, and we slowed as we passed Mount Hope cemetery and I heard Arturo mumbling something I could not make out. I saw him make the sign of the cross as we passed by.

Soon after, we turned into an alley and parked behind an old Spanish mission. The two of us were told to get out of the vehicle and scan the area around the building. Once done we would then go inside, do the same and once clear one of us would return to the car for Arturo and Javier. We did as we were told and noticed nothing out of the ordinary around the building.

Of course, if it were an ambush or something the vehicles would likely roll in once we were inside. These guys were not complete idiots, just criminals.

We were shown into a smaller room, dark and dusty. It smelled like a moldy old library. The two men in the room waiting for us made a big deal about removing their weapons and directed us to do the same. I figured it was standard operating procedure, so I did that but kept my knife. We then went out to the car and told Javier everything was good. Javier opened a secret compartment in the vehicle and handed Bobby two MAC-10's with four clips. The Mac-10's hung on straps under his arms, one on each side. He would remain outside to keep an eye on things.

The MAC 10 is a compact machine pistol that can fire close to twenty-three rounds per second. I could see by the clips that these were chambered in .45 ACP calibre. That was a large shell with a ton of stopping power. You could easily cut a vehicle in half with two of those, much less a body or two. You had to have a lot of strength to be able to hold and fire those in one hand.

I felt oddly safer knowing that Bobby had our backs, armed to the teeth.

The three of us were soon in the same small room and Javier and Arturo were asked to open their jackets and be inspected. I had no idea who we were meeting but I now knew he was likely equal in status to Arturo.

We were then escorted through a door in the back of the room. Two men sat at a table and two more stood behind them.

On the drive over Javier had warned us about everything that would happen prior to the meeting. The weapons, search and all the rest of it. He said that once in that room the other side may or may not have weapons, but we should act as if they did. I was starting to think this was a high visibility hit. They would leave one survivor to relate to the others how this big boss was so easily eliminated.

That was one of the ways that these higher-level dealers absorbed territories and business from the competition. Consider it the ultimate hostile takeover. No stock purchase, no board meetings, no negotiation. A simple annihilation of the top "executives" and now you owned the company.

During Javier's explanation on the drive here he said that when Arturo used the words "Los negocios son Buenos" (business is good) we were to pounce. Obviously, the meeting was not expected to last long, so I wondered why the secrecy, why not just take them out? I supposed mine was not to question why.

Arturo sat at the table alone while we flanked him. Javier knew the other men would be like this as the man on Hector's side always sat next to him. It was rumored he never left Hector's side, ever. When the words were spoken, Javier would take out the guy across from him and I would take out the standing and seated ones across from me. He knew from past displays that I could easily handle them both and maybe even all three without Arturo getting hurt.

Arturo asked quite a few questions and the other guy did a lot of talking. Arturo must have all the information he needed as he uttered the word for which we were waiting. We sprang into action and all hell broke loose. I had been able to get my knife into my hand and knew how I would move. Across the table I flew at the same time as Javier. I was focused on my guys, so I couldn't see what Javier was doing.

I sunk the knife deep into the seated guy and hit the button. I felt him explode out the front of his body and left the knife as I struck the other guy. He was a little more agile and stronger than I expected but he was still no match for me. We exchanged blows at close quarters and when he thought he had me I sent a vicious strike up into his jaw. He collapsed like a sack of potatoes and was out cold. I watched as Javier wiped off his knife on his victim's own jacket and replaced it from where he retrieved it. His victim had a deep slice running the full width of his neck, air still gurgling out of him through the bloody mess where his throat used to be.

Javier then came around, reached down, and grabbed my guy's ponytail and lifted him up. He dropped him into a chair after disarming him completely and then we waited with the two of them. Arturo was still seated, staring calmly at Hector. Two of his men dead on either side of him and the third now seated next to him. I knew his head was still spinning and he probably couldn't even focus his eyes. I had hit him hard enough to have killed him but there he sat. One tough hombre. I retrieved my own knife out of dead guy # 1, cleaned it off and slipped it back into the padded sock.

As the ponytail guy came to, he realized what was going on and simply sat still, comprehending it was over. Javier stood next to Hector, grabbed the gun he had removed from the other guy and held it to Hector's temple. Arturo folded his hands in front of him, looked across the table at the guy with the ponytail and very calmly said, "Tu jefe esta muerto." (your boss is dead). He added, "Su jefe esta muerto." (his boss is dead). In English he told him that you will relay the message that I now own this organization. I own you and I will let you run the operation provided you are loyal. If I have ANY concerns, you will meet the same end as Hector.

That was when Javier pulled the trigger of the .44 and blew Hector's brains all over his own guy's head. The whole room was an absolute mess. There was blood and guts everywhere.

The guy I used my knife on was blown wide open and the ponytail dude was sitting in his own entrails. Javier's target created a massive blood pool that continued to spread. We stood to leave, and Arturo offered his hand to the man whose boss had just been assassinated. They shook hands and Arturo looked into his eyes and said, "I hope I can trust you. I am growing tired of all the bloodshed."

Ponytail guy swore his loyalty and said he would deliver the whole organization and they would be pleased to work for such a successful boss.

Arturo added that he would not touch the families of the dead men in the room but added that if he did not remain loyal, he would have them all killed. He would then make this guy watch as his own family, including his daughters, were all killed. He looked at Arturo and guaranteed he would never have to do that.

Once again, the mere threat of violence would get the job done. Certainly, with a guy like this as it was clear he wanted no more killing. I hoped Arturo had no intention of killing innocent people as I would have no choice but to protect them. I may have reset my moral compass but had not thrown it out completely yet!

We retrieved our guns, left the building, and returned to the SUV. We drove in a very law-abiding manner back to the compound and I was told to shower and return to the table outside.

Despite our murderous and messy activities, it was another beautiful warm night in La Jolla and apparently, they boys wanted to relax.

I showered off the mess and had to shampoo my short hair twice to get all the blood out. I wanted to scrub myself raw and didn't know why. I had certainly done worse. Heck, I had done worse to my own Bobby as punishment for his transgressions. Somehow this was different for me. It appeared Hector had simply fallen from favor, or he had chosen the wrong guy to compete with. Either way, it seemed like overkill to me and that was something with which I was familiar.

One of the staff brought out a couple of bottles of wine. Javier poured a glass for each of us, and Arturo raised his and toasted us. He said he was impressed again by my skill and awfully glad he had found me before anyone else did. He looked at me and asked if I had any idea what this evening meant to our organization? I said more business, less competition and he said, "no, no. What does it mean in dollars?" I told him I couldn't even hazard a guess as I had no idea what that stuff sells for.

He smiled a huge smile at the both of us, raised his glass once more and said, "here's to another million." I said wow, another million a year is a lot of cash. Both Arturo and Javier laughed loudly as Arturo said, "no, no my dear, a million a month...or more."

I supposed that did make sense as I was currently sipping the best, and I was certain most expensive, wine I had ever tasted. Jonathon and Kathy had some great wines and clearly plenty of cash to buy the best, but this was a step up from that. It was utterly amazing. I would roll a bit around in my mouth, inject a little air and then let it slide slowly down my throat. Deep red in color and with just enough oak to give it some character it was an amazing bottle of wine.

Javier drained the balance of the first bottle into our glasses and Arturo added, "plenty more where that came from. Tonight, we celebrate." I sipped slowly on mine and neither of them noticed they were drinking at better than a two to one clip versus me. I wasn't about to become inebriated and risk anything going wrong now. I had gotten into the organization and successfully gained at least some trust.

Now it was time for the next phase.

I knew I needed something dramatic to vault me past Arturo and hopefully a step closer to El Rey. I needed to ensure Javier remained whole too. That way Arturo would not have as big an issue if he had to "give me up" to his boss.

Chapter Twenty 6 – Saving Arturo

Now it was time to really step things up. I needed to meet with Colin, so we could discuss the best way to have me recognized further up the food chain. I had some ideas but needed to ensure we were in synch. Monitoring by Colin would be critical to success in this next phase.

We went about the next few days, business as usual. Ponytail guy, I found out his name was Roberto, came over during the week. I was in the background and Javier never left Arturo's side as they discussed details with their newest recruit. He seemed remarkably calm sitting down with the two people who assassinated two of his coworkers and blasted his own boss's brains all over his face only days earlier.

I wondered how every one of these guys wasn't suffering from some form of PTSD. I suppose, perhaps they were. They lived such a dangerous and singular existence. At least in the forces you knew you could rely on the person next to you. These guys didn't even have that. They could rely only on themselves and a lot of them seemed ill-equipped to even do that!

I waited until Thursday to hit the gym as according to our schedule, Colin would be at home in the morning. I went through my usual steps and was soon heading North on I-5 in that stupid little Civic.

I would feel a lot safer on my bike or in my truck but that would be even more dangerous. I listened to my favorite play list as I motored up the highway with seemingly millions of others.

Seven lanes wide at this point and every lane packed with vehicles. I wondered how far away from that island existence I was. I had never really considered such a thing but when I used it as a cover and then found out I had a net worth of more than four million it became a little more real to me. I was not about to do anything crazy, but it was good to have some other options.

After cranking through my favorite tunes, I found myself on Colin's driveway. A double honk and the garage door opened. I parked the little car and went inside. We hugged, and Colin offered me a fruit smoothie which I gladly accepted.

We sat in his office while I detailed the last few days events for him. I explained that I think we still needed the fake robbery, or even a fake attempt on Arturo's life. As we looked at the board and all our notes, we decided that an attempt on Arturo's life would be our best option. Colin said the message traffic he had been monitoring indicated that El Rey and Arturo were closer than we thought.

If there was an attempt on Arturo's life and I saved him while Javier was unharmed that would be the best option. I needed Javier to still be Arturo's "guy" in hopes I could get plucked by the next guy up the chain. We were hoping that next guy might be El Rey, or someone directly connected to him. We knew I needed to be IN Mexico to be able to further our plan.

Although it would cost Arturo his beloved boat, we began to think the best approach would be a raid. If we left it up to the Coast Guard, we determined we would have the best chance of us escaping. The only problem is the submarine only held two people. I told Colin there was scuba gear as well, using rebreathers, so travelling just below the surface and away from propellers and such I could go miles. Whomever was in the scuba gear would leave the same way as the submarine.

The boat was equipped with sophisticated sonar and radar with ship identification software. It was the same software used by the coast guard and the navy. If someone did not spot the boat(s) approaching I could blow the whistle provided I was close to the radar panels. I could then get Arturo and Javier below decks and out via the submarine while I grabbed the scuba gear and dry suit.

It would make a compelling story as I would be sure to force Javier to go with Arturo as he would need the protection. They would be impressed with my apparent selflessness and then with my skills in the water.

Navy SEALS are seriously well-trained. They could certainly swim and dive in all conditions. For their Basic Underwater Demolition/ SEAL training (BUD/S) they developed a technique known as the Combat Swimmer Stroke. It is performed mostly underwater, rather than on the surface, and is a combination of breaststroke, freestyle and sidestroke that enables them to swim miles while conserving energy.

It combines a scissor stroke that orients the body sideways in the water. This tilts your body so one arm is slightly higher than the other and you pull that arm back to propel yourself forward. Your other arm remains outstretched and then you pull that one down as you begin another scissor kick. Not only does it help to swim long distances it also makes the person difficult to spot underwater, looking more like a large fish than a human. This stroke helps conserve energy so that when you land, after however many miles you swim, you are still combat ready.

That is why the SEAL pin, the trident, is also called the Budweiser. The swimming requirement is core to becoming a seal and the trident nickname plays on that BUD'S acronym.

The Budweiser means so much to SEALs it is one of the very few military badges issued in only one grade. Officers and enlisted personnel are recognized as equals.

As great as those guys are, I have had the same training. I also took it to the next level and use Zen-like breathing techniques that give me an edge on even our vaunted SEALS. Don't get me wrong, I love and respect those guys, but I still have an edge. I do everything I can to retain that edge, so I knew I could accomplish this.

SEALs are also wicked good shooters. Chris Kyle (the guy the movie American Sniper was based on) admitted that his record breaking 2,100-yard sniper shot was "straight up luck". By contrast, there was no luck when a Canadian sniper eliminated an IS militant from over 3,835 yards away!

Kyle used a TAC 338 rifle and the Canadian used a TAC 50.

Still the McMillan TAC 50, according to the manufacturer, has an effective range of just under 2,000 yards. That makes a 3,835-yard shot that much more impressive. The US Navy SEALS now use the same rifle for sniper duty although that one is called the MK 15.

My sniper skills were more along the lines of the Chris Kyle distance but that is still damn good.

Especially when you consider I am always operating without a spotter. I laugh when I see those movies where the boys are all celebrating when some clown hits the small circle at 500 or 600 yards. I'm confident that even without using a .50 cal that I could go ten of ten in the circle and most likely seven of ten straight through the bullseye.

I always thought I would have made a great operating SEAL, so I kept an eye out for what they were doing. Ultimately, as far as our government was concerned, I could help our cause much more where I was put. I probably agree with them, knowing what I know now. Nevertheless, there were times where I felt I could have really used the camaraderie and support of other SEALs. Plus, they were a fun bunch of guys to hang with when you're not working.

Colin and I reviewed all the details of the plan. The date and time would need to be fluid and we would not have a ton of time to warn them. Luckily, Colin and I could stay connected other ways. I had tapped into a different wireless network close to Arturo's and I could send the encrypted information from there. We had the plan detailed and Colin was going to make some preliminary contact.

Fortunately, he had an in with the Coast Guard in the area as a friend of his was a senior officer.

Colin could use that relationship to get things ready and then to pull the trigger when we were ready. Even without Arturo, it would be a big win to capture the drugs and a boat. I would continue with things as usual and watch and wait for our opportunity.

I reversed my tracks, picked up my vehicle and headed back to the compound knowing I had a solid plan and the best of backup. While I monitored our own situation, Colin began working with his Coast Guard buddy.

When I returned, the whole team had a dinner together and I will admit I liked it. In another time, or perhaps another world, these guys could have been my teammates. Had I have chosen to become a thief or drug person they would have been my team of SEALS.

.

Chapter Twenty 7- The Coast Guard

Things were a little uneventful and I wondered if maybe Arturo was planning to lay low for a while. That would be too bad as I was ready to go, I wanted to get to the next level. I knew you could not rush these things but that couldn't stop me from getting anxious!

Things went as usual for the next couple of weeks. I had been a driver more often than not as Arturo felt that was the best cover for me. It was easier to explain me as a driver than just someone along for the ride, looking like a lawyer. The thing I did notice is that Arturo was much more active than I thought when I first met him. Typically, the higher-level guys were never out and about as much as Arturo was. I chalked it up to the trust issues they all had and not an if you want it done right, do it yourself motto.

There were a couple of dustups during the waiting time. It was more like one dust-up and another sneak attack. I witnessed Arturo's ruthlessness up close and personal. I think it was him keeping up his street cred but also to send a message to the whole team. One of his contacts had screwed up big time. He tried to cover up a little doing his own business through another supplier, but that sort of thing was tough to disguise.

I was warned it was black tie and got prepared. I drove, with Javier and Arturo in the back. In comparison to Mount Hope (or Mount Hopeless as the residents often refer to it) it appeared we were headed to a nicer area.

On the surface, Pacific Beach appeared to be a typical quaint little beach-side community.

The crime stats for the area told a much different story. It is only slightly better than East Village, the top of the heap for crime in San Diego. At two rapes per month and an assault or aggravated assault every two days, Pacific Beach was nowhere near as quaint as it appeared. There are lots of property crimes, car thefts and other crimes too.

As we drove up Grand Avenue, through the center of Pacific Beach I was briefed on what was going to happen. We were going to park around the corner and meet three guys at the PB shore club. The leader, Curtis, was the only one who would be taken out. Arturo would do it while we kept the other two from joining in. We parked and walked around the corner.

It was an odd little joint. A one level bar/restaurant above a small market. You accessed it via an outside set of stairs that fronted on the beach but there was another hidden set of stairs in the back. We went around to the back and used those stairs. We walked up the rickety wooden steps gingerly as they didn't feel all that solid. Salt air tends to do that to unprotected wood.

We reached the top and Javier knocked on the door and a small hole in the door slid open so whomever was inside could decide whether to unlock or not. I heard three locks opening and we were led directly into what appeared to be a stock room.

The fellow took us to the back of the room where the other two were seated at a table. It was to be a friendly discussion with a regular customer so, although I'm sure they were all carrying, nobody was on high alert. It was a round table and the way everyone sat it made our task quite simple.

Curtis was across from Arturo, flanked by two guys who looked like college athletes. Apparently these two were Curtis' version of me and Javier. They could have been football players or something I supposed but I was confident they would be no match for us. The chat started out with generalities about their business and that type of thing.

When Arturo gave the signal, Javier and I moved next to each of our guys, pulling weapons as we did. In a second, we each had a pistol pressed into the back of the neck of each guy and a second one pointed at Curtis. Arturo slowly stood up and asked Curtis if he liked the product he had been getting from us? Curtis blubbered out a yes, of course. Arturo was now behind him with a hand on his shoulder and quietly asked why he was buying product elsewhere then?

A scared little boy look slowly emerged on Curtis' face. He started to speak, and Arturo told him to shut up and listen. My guy went to move, and I whipped him in the head with my pistol and pushed him down into his seat. Javier told them the only one in trouble here was Curtis. They could choose to sit and watch, and then be released unharmed or they could be killed. The choice was theirs.

They chose wisely. I watched Arturo reach into his pocket, and I knew there would be no shooting tonight. When I spotted the wire, I knew immediately he was going to use my favorite weapon, the garotte. Sure enough, I watched him remove his other hand from Curtis' shoulder and grab one wooden handle while the other remained in his left hand.

The wire was braided so was not designed for a quick and bloody kill. This was simply a matter of a slower strangulation. Arturo made the loop and dropped it over Curtis' head, settling it onto his neck right above the adams apple. He pulled his hands apart quickly and Curtis was unable to make any noise. I watched as he grasped at the wire, but it was already too tight for him to get his fingers underneath it. I knew it would not have helped anyway but the victim always tried.

The whole time Curtis was choking, struggling to get even the smallest breath, Arturo kept up a quiet running commentary.

He softly said he never liked to do this, but he always demanded 100% loyalty from all his people and customers. He locked eyes with the other two as the life slowly left Curtis, his eyes bugging out now and his skin glowing red. He slumped down but Arturo held him up by the throat, the garotte easing him closer and closer to death with each passing second.

We just stood with our guns still pointed at his two guys until Arturo was done. He let Curtis head drop to the table when he was sure he was gone, removed the garotte and returned it to his pocket. He sat down in his original seat and told the two guys they needed to commit to a choice, right here and right now. They could take over the business and have the freedom to talk to anyone, except the police of course, about what they saw here today. They could also choose to walk away from the business, still free to tell the story. If they made the disastrous third choice to go back to the other supplier or try something stupid, they would both be killed.

Arturo then laid out the volumes and prices that he had been supplying Curtis with. The two boys quickly did the math and indicated they wanted to take over. They professed undying loyalty to Arturo and said they would never use any other supplier. All the usual stuff one would expect to hear.

Arturo said they would have to maintain the same volume for three months.

At the end of that three months, their regular buy would be increased by 20%. He knew that they were making good profit and in the worst-case scenario they would simply be paying more and likely having an oversupply until they caught up. Of course, the real worst-case scenario would be that they were unable to increase the volume and eventually Arturo would have them disposed of, reclaim the product, and find someone else. It was the ultimate sales eat what you kill scenario.

They each shook hands with Arturo, we put away our weapons and calmly took the back stairs again. After we got into the car Arturo just said it had been a long night and we should get home. As we drove, I overheard them talking about a pickup next week.

Javier suggested taking me out on the Arturo for a night-time sail.

I went immediately into planning mode when I heard Arturo say that he was going too, and they would need a full complement of security. I knew I would need to contact Colin immediately so that he could have his coast guard buddy on alert. It would be critical that Arturo, Javier, and I were all positioned properly, when the coast guard was spotted, to have the plan work.

I parked the car and we all decided to turn in. No wine, no ocean watching. It had been a tough night and although Arturo was cool as a cucumber, I'm sure there was some stress beneath the surface. I said I needed a hot shower and headed straight to my room. A couple of the boys were watching TV as I walked past, nobody saying anything.

I went into the bathroom, locked the door, and turned the water on. I grabbed the burner phone and sent a quick message to Colin, using the other wireless network. I let him know the plan was imminent and I would likely be able to give him only one- or two-hours notice. The tiny tracker I had hidden on the boat would guide them. He acknowledged me, and I shut the phone down and returned it to its hiding place.

I had a very relaxing hot shower, the room got so steamed up that you couldn't see your hand in front of your face. It felt good to just let the water warm me all over and take a few isolated minutes thinking of nothing.

I thought it might be good to watch a little tube so after I dried off, I got into some sweatpants and sweatshirt and went out to hang with the boys. We had a beer and didn't talk too much as we watched the Chargers playing.

Even though they had moved to Los Angeles in many ways, the Chargers were still San Diego's team. The boys were excited as we watched them kick the crap out of the Buffalo Bills. It was sort of like our own private sports bar.

I didn't last too long as I really was wiped out, so I went to bed as soon as I finished my beer. I figured it was important to stay connected to the crew and this was the easiest way to ensure I was just one of the boys.

I was already looking forward to a nice long run in the morning. It was always sunny and warm, and it was a terrific opportunity to both clear my head and plan for the days ahead. I found I had acute focus when I ran like this, my body operating at top efficiency, and it seemed to supercharge my mind at the same time.

Chapter Twenty 8 – The Daring Escape

A couple of days later Javier said we should head over to the boat as we needed to review some things. We drove over to the marina and walked down the dock. It moved ever so slightly as the waves rolled into shore on yet another bright, sunny day in San Diego. I had been here a few times now, but I was still blown away by the sheer opulence of some of these boat and yachts. Each one reeking of luxury and wealth.

There was a mix of sailing yachts (like Arturo's) , motor yachts and power boats that boggled the mind. I was amazed as I walked down the dock and looked at a powerboat that was made by Mystic. The name was covered but there was a slogan on the side of the boat, close to the stern, which said "When the flag drops, the bullshit stops!" I suppose that was taking the "mine's bigger than yours" idiom right to the max. Boys and their phallic-replacement toys.

I spoke to a fellow who was on it one day and he told me they were made in Florida, and this was the fastest boat on the water, capable of more than two hundred miles per hour. This one had two turbine engines that produce 2,050 horsepower each. I knew cars and bikes and there was no comparison to something that had over 4,000 HP.

It was about fifty feet long and a catamaran hull but even with that, there was no way I would want to be in one of those things.

Me and Javier didn't really talk much until we got onto the boat. Once we boarded, it was just us, and Javier began sharing details. We would be making a pick-up, but Arturo's main contact was planning to meet us there.

He reviewed where Arturo would spend most of the trip, with Javier in his usual spot right outside that door. I would maintain overwatch on them both and monitor what was going on around us. It was the ideal setup, and I could not have drawn it up better myself. We went through emergency procedures, including how to launch the pods in case that was necessary.

He explained how the pods were shaped a little like sharks and that they were propelled by electric motors. Even with sonar tracking the boat it would appear as if a couple of sharks were cutting across underneath. It was an amazing setup. We reviewed the escape procedures including the sub and the scuba rebreather gear. I have to say, he was very thorough, and I felt as prepared as I was before any mission. We finished and he said we would be leaving the slip at 6:00 PM on Thursday.

We would look like your typical sunset cruise that was so popular in that area at this time of year. There would be boats everywhere likely but most of the smaller ones would head back to dock as soon as the sun set.

Boats like that were not usually equipped to be out on the open water overnight like us. Arturo's craft has all the electronics, sonar, radar and even doppler weather tracking that would keep us safe. Advance warning of any marine event was always key to survival on the ocean.

We left the boat and drove back to the compound in relative silence.

There really wasn't anything to discuss and it's not like we had to maintain small talk or anything. I was looking forward to a good workout and maybe some sparring too. Going to the gym would also allow me to connect with Colin. I could simply pass along the information electronically, but I really wanted to just say hello too.

The next day I awoke, had a protein shake, and went straight to the gym. I was powering through an excellent workout when Colin arrived. He was at the station behind me, and I told him we were going out Thursday. No idea where, but he could use the tracker to find out. I knew it was meant to look like two friends meeting in the ocean to party on their boats, so we would be together for at least a few hours. I finished my workout and went directly back to the compound. Now was not the time to do anything out of the ordinary, at least my current ordinary.

When I returned and parked, Javier and Arturo were sitting out at the table and Javier motioned me over. Javier told me to sit and asked if I wanted some fresh fruit. Arturo seemed to be sipping on a pitcher of sangria.

I thought it a little early in the day for that but there was fruit in there too. I supposed it might be viewed as healthy wine when you considered that.

It was just general conversation really. A little bit about being ready for Thursday evening, asking if I needed Dramamine to be on the boat that long. The usual stuff you might ask someone who did not have my skills and training. I laughed most of it off and said I was always ready, and I think they both knew that.

A little braggadocio with guys like this always went a long way toward fitting in. In my world, I WAS the 4,000 plus HP fastest boat in the water. I was proud of that. Proud of what I had done for my country. We finished our chat, and I went to my room to relax and destress for a while. I knew Thursday evening would arrive too soon and I would have to be sharp and ready for anything. I felt my plan was solid and would work but there were a lot of moving parts, so I would have to be extra vigilant.

It seemed to take forever, but also happen quickly, when Thursday arrived. Javier and I went down to check over the boat and do one final review. There were crew already there preparing for what looked like a large party. Javier explained that the cover was a party, so all the security guys would be well dressed, not carrying, and have "dates" with them.

I suggested that was a lot of different people in the mix, adding hookers in might not be a great idea. Javier said they had all been vetted, had been used before and had no idea what was really going on. To anyone who got close, or the authorities, it was just another party. I suppose with all the wealthy people and cash that made sense however, with "Arturo from La Jolla" stencilled on the back of the boat, I wondered how effective all the misdirection would really be.

My security mates started to show up, each paired with a woman. I was sure they were the best-looking women these guys would ever be seen with. It was like that first day around the pool with a bunch of Bond-girls or Robert Palmer video women showing up. There were four "couples" in all including the best of the best for Arturo. Javier said, for public consumption that I would be his date. Provided he wasn't stupid enough to expect me to sleep with him I said that would be fine. Business is business.

We were sailing out to meet Arturo's boss, who I now knew was El Rey de Los Muertos. Finally, I may come face to face, or at least be within one hundred yards of the man who was my ultimate target. It was another enjoyable day to be on the water.

Soon, everyone was on the boat, and we motored away from our slip and out into the open ocean.

The wind was favorable, and thankfully light, and soon the engines were shut off and the sails raised. It was quite the feeling to be slipping quietly through the cerulean blue waves, watching as they broke to either side of the bow. The ride, if that's what they call it, was like a big Cadillac rolling down the highway. It felt smooth, substantial, and very stable. I watched the crew go quietly about their various jobs, each one performing like an Olympic athlete.

As the sunset got closer, we all moved to the rear of the boat and were seated around a large table and bar. Altogether, there were twelve of us and it looked like a typical rich people party on the water. As we milled around, and got seated, champagne was brought to the table.

Arturo gave quite a little speech, showing off his knowledge. As our glasses were filled, he said this was a 2006 Pannier and was one of the finest champagnes in the world. He explained that its hints of lemon, honey, and grilled nuts along with a very fresh and dry finish made it special. He chuckled and said that the bourgeois yuppies and grill-wearing gang bangers can drink all the Cristal and Dom they like but that swill was all crap compared to this. They were also more than two and three times the price.

He went on to explain, as we all sipped, that too often quality was connected only to price. What we were drinking recently scored ninety-seven points out of a possible one hundred in a prestigious international champagne competition. The best palates in the world determined this to be the best champagne.

He seemed to really enjoy this part of the evening. I was positive most of the people had heard it all, or something similar, before but nevertheless feigned interest. I guessed that was part of the job too, everyone has to blow a little smoke up their boss's butt to keep him or her happy.

We were then served the most amazing seafood. Platters of crab, lobster, shellfish and more filled the table. All prepared differently with something for everyone. Arturo looked at these events, even though everyone was working, as a way to say thank you to his people. He seemed to enjoy sharing his wealth in this way. Of course, these people had or would save his life repeatedly, so he was well advised to ensure they were happy.

We ate to our hearts content, although I kept it light as I knew I had to swim at least five miles at some point this evening. I had the one glass of champagne but filled my glass with water after that.

The sun began to set and, even though the circumstances weren't exactly relaxing, it was amazing to see. I never tired of watching the changing colors bouncing off the tops of the small waves and across the face of the dark ocean as the sun slowly sank lower. Bright red and orange flame-like tendrils shooting off the water as the sun put on an otherworldly display. I just never tired of that event, each one offering distinct colors and light from the night before. Clouds often adding a different view. There were no clouds tonight. It was smooth and quiet. I really hoped it stayed that way as although I could swim in anything I would prefer a nice, calm swim to shore.

I was on the front deck with Javier when he looked ahead and said there she is. Even as the sun was setting, I could see the ominous-looking craft slipping through the waves towards us. It had huge sails, illuminated by bright lights, and a dark blue or black hull. It resembled a large submarine more than a sailing yacht. The closer it got the more sinister and the larger it appeared.

It looked so sleek and fast as it smoothly and effortlessly moved through the dark ocean. Our crew had deployed large, inflatable bumpers all along the sides of our boat. Each one looked like two

45-gallon drums stacked on top of each other. I supposed when you had a boat like this one a few extra bumpers couldn't hurt. As the other craft got closer its sails were lowered and they slowed to a snail's pace. You could see they had deployed the same type of bumpers on theirs.

The crew on each craft were scurrying across the decks with ropes and cables seemingly everywhere. Soon, both boats were connected, the bumpers keeping the hulls apart and ropes holding the two together as if it were one huge catamaran.

I would come to know this yacht was called the Ngoni. Its very appropriate nickname was the beast. A high-performance sloop. A sailing yacht like no other. A smooth carbon fibre hull topped by curving glass panels that retract into the roof to bring the outside inside. I also learned it was just shy of 190 feet long.

El Rey had purchased her from a fellow named Tony Buckingham, an oil baron who had also been a partner in a global "security" firm. I wondered what their connection was. Those security firms, especially the ones operating overseas, frequently employed ex CIA, law enforcement and other security force type folks.

There was a gangplank secured between the two craft and I watched as Arturo and Javier went to the plank. They crossed to the other boat and within minutes I could hear that Arturo was not happy. I heard him yell, "Donde esta el? Donde esta el?" (Where is he?) There was quieter discussion and they both returned. Neither looked happy. Javier barked at the boys to get the product and load up the pods as quickly as they could.

I heard Javier ask Arturo what happened to El Rey, where was he? He said he was told that something came up. He could not make it and they had to get rid of the product they had. I figured something was certainly up but there was no way to call off the raid now. The Coast guard would be coming soon.

Arturo and Javier went to his room to discuss as two pods were fully loaded with what looked like heroin. I felt a vibration in my shoe and that was the signal the coast guard was on its way. El Rey's boat was clean but ours was now loaded with millions of dollars worth of heroin. The execution of the next part of my plan had to be flawless. Luckily, before Javier went below deck, he told me to keep my eyes peeled.

I went to the communications room and saw there were two boats steaming our way. The software told us they were most likely Coast Guard medium Response Boats. They were about forty-five feet long and powered by two 1,650 HP diesel engines. They were no Mystic speedboats, but they were capable of almost eighty miles per hour (42 knots). One of them could tow a 100-ton vessel in rough waters and they were equipped with two .50 caliber machine guns.

With six crew on each they were a formidable assault team. As soon as I spotted them, I raised the alarm. I went below deck and laid out the situation to Javier. He told me to get the pods out. Send a man to each of the two heroin-filled pods and dump them. I looked at him and said that he and Arturo should leave now in the sub. It would be safest. I said there must be something up because how would the Coast Guard know where to find us? Why would they think there was anything illegal going on? It was all too strange. With them gone, it would just be the guys having a party on their boss's boat.

Javier agreed it would be safest if they did leave and asked what I would do. I told him it wouldn't be good for me to be found with the crew and that I would swim to shore. He looked at me with an incredulous look on his face and asked if I knew how far it was. I said it appeared to be between five and seven miles, but I could handle it.

He wished me luck and the two of them scrambled out the back hatch and down the passageway to the sub. I raced up top and got the pods launched away from the boat.

The guys knew they were to say they were just partying on their boss's boat at his request. A reward for working so hard. The Coast Guard could board but they would find nothing. The Ngoni was already moving away quickly, sails up and headed back to sovereign waters off Mexico.

There were no lights illuminating those huge sails now, she was simply a silent black behemoth easing into the darkness. I ensured everything was good, areas around the pods were being cleaned and the decks were being hosed off. I went back below decks and raced down the passageway. I got into the wetsuit as I figured I would overheat in a dry suit; the waters were not that cold. I pulled on the scuba gear, slipped my feet into the flippers, and eased myself out the back of the boat.

I was very quickly far from the boat, using the combat stroke and staying underwater, about twenty feet below the surface. I was safely out of propeller range and knew I was not in a shipping lane. I was well equipped for the swim with a GPS watch, three WASP knives and my wits.

It was unlikely I would run into sharks at this time in these waters, but I still had to be vigilant. Thankfully, it was a very high-tech mask. It had some sort of mini sonar setup that would display what was in my field of view.

I kept moving toward my mark as I cleared my mind, and focused on easy breathing, easy swimming, and a comfortable pace. That was the big advantage of the combat stroke. You could swim close to or on the surface and go seemingly forever. I was already in a zone of calmness, almost like before taking a sniper shot. My heart rate was a little higher than would be required to shoot steadily at a far away target, but it was perfect for what I was doing.

I was now almost two miles from the boat and was considering ditching the re-breather, but I decided against it. If I did have to avoid something, not having that gear would be a huge impediment. It was worth the extra drag in the water to have that as insurance. I would ditch it, along with my weight belt when I was about a mile from shore. I just kept focussed, stuck to my pace and was happy that I did not have to avoid anything substantial like a Coast Guard craft or a shark!

As much as three wasp knives made me feel a little safer, they would be of little use against a pack of sharks. One or two I would likely be safer as the others would follow the one stabbed and about to explode all the way to the surface. I could never outswim a shark, no human could, so defense was everything. Distraction was important too.

I glanced at my watch and noticed I was approaching the distance from which I wanted to free swim. Tick, tick, tick the display changed slowly until it wound down to less than one mile. I removed my belt, lashed it to the breathing apparatus and let the unit fill with water. I released it to the bottom, and it sank quickly as I swam away. I had spotted a light on shore to keep an eye on and headed towards that.

With swim fins on and no re-breather on my back I felt like I was racing through the water.

I felt like I was Michael, freaking, Phelps as I flew effortlessly through the darkness. I wanted to make a game out of it by this point so I decided when I was a half mile offshore, I would sprint in. No combat stroke, just a good old-fashioned crawl. A race to the finish line.

I waited for the watch to signal a half mile out and then I put my head down and really started pounding. The larger than average, Navy SEAL swim fins propelled me forward at an amazing pace. In no time, I felt the warm sand against my stomach and then I was standing on shore. There was a pickup vehicle that had the coordinates of my watch. The sub would go back and sit on the bottom at the end of the dock. The water was only about twenty feet deep but that was more than enough to conceal the sub and not be in anyone's way.

Arturo and Javier would use a couple of compact air bottles, crawl out the airlock and surface to a waiting boat. I would get out of my wetsuit, bag it up with my fins and wait until they came to get me. It was a nice night, but I was hoping they wouldn't take too long as I was looking forward to a beer and a rest!

I had only waited about forty-five minutes when a car pulled into the lot above the highway. I watched until they flashed the code and then I ran up the beach and jumped into the car, tossing my stuff into the trunk.

We drove back to the compound and when we arrived Javier and Arturo were cleaned up and having a drink. They suggested I go inside and change and then come on back to the table. I said I needed to shower too and took my time.

I needed to be sure I was completely calm. I had to be ready as, being the new guy, I would likely be under suspicion.

Chapter Twenty 9 – A Mole In The Coast Guard?

I walked calmly out the back door and headed to the table. Javier asked if I wanted a beer and grabbed me one from the fridge. As I sat, he looked at me and said that was close. I said it sure was but glad we were all safe. I confirmed what I had hoped, the Coast Guard boarded, found nothing, and had no reasonable cause to search and that was that.

Arturo said he got a phone call from his boss when they got back to the house. He said that he had received word of a possible raid by the Coast Guard. He claimed it was too late for him to warn Arturo. They all carried phones of course but he also knew their regular phones were likely being monitored. The DEA and DHS had a lot of stroke with judges and they could almost do whatever they wished.

Now I had two large problems. The first that Colin's contact might get burned for coming up with a dry hole after activating two pursuit boats with a total of twelve men. The second that this mole could be anyone in the Coast Guard. Even worse, it could be Colin's guy. I didn't think so, but anything was possible in this world.

Javier quizzed me about when I found Alonzo. Did I have any idea how long he had been on the boat? Was I sure there was only one tracker?

I told him we both did a sweep and didn't find anything else so how could there be. I knew that Javier would do everything but strip that boat down to the spars the next day.

I also knew there WAS another tracker, and it was the same kind that I had "caught" Alonzo planting. They really needed to find it and I was glad I was not bothered with that task. Javier sent the full team down there soon after they moored. I waited and tried to be calm and finally, after almost four hours, one of the guys came up to Javier and dropped something into his hand.

After he walked away, he slammed it down onto the table. Just as I thought he was about to yell at me he spat out a stream of Spanish pejoratives ending with Alonzo. He couldn't believe there was a second one we had not found. He also could not understand how Alonzo could have been on the Coast Guard payroll. They both said how we would need to be incredibly careful going forward. I supposed that, since they saw me kill more than one man, they knew I couldn't be an agent. That was the benefit of doing this the way we were doing it.

A simple U/C or C/I would likely have been sniffed out by now. Because I had killed, there was no way I could be connected.

They knew their law as, if I was on a police payroll, I couldn't go as far as killing someone to get inside. I would then be just as guilty as they were. We reviewed every person and I noted myself as one of the newbies, before they could. They both laughed and said they had enough on me to have me put away for three lifetimes. I was unsure what exactly they had, or if they were bluffing, but that comment was the two of them signing their own death warrant.

I now knew I would have to take them both out. I would need to dispose of El Rey first, otherwise it would look a little suspicious. I hoped my bravery and quick thinking on this raid was enough to have El Rey eventually ask about me. After all, I spotted the two boats on the radar and took the hard way out while Arturo and Javier were able to get away cleanly. The drugs were safe at the bottom of the ocean and in a few more days the trackers would self activate. We just had to wait at the surface in the boat, trigger the inflation of the floats, and wait patiently while the booty surfaced.

There was a system of matched electromagnets that would guide the pods right back to the hatches from which they emerged a few days ago. It really was quite the setup.

Overall, everything ended well.

Chapter 30 – Business

The next few weeks were all about business. The pods had been recovered and underlings had taken care of the deliveries. The boat had a new electronic sweeper system installed that made it impossible to track, or carry something that could track, its movements. From here on out absolutely everyone was scanned as they boarded. Cell phones and any other devices were collected and locked into a lead lined safe, after the batteries were removed, just to be extra safe.

Although it was an inconvenience, I thought that it might help me at some point. Knowing they had no method of communicating, other than ship to shore radio might help me achieve one or more of my goals.

Since that last shipment was clearly a "save" everyone was rewarded with a bonus payment. The boys were all celebrating but I had not yet received mine, so I was a little concerned. I worried that I may be under suspicion.

Javier sent someone in, and I was summoned to the table. When I got there and sat down Arturo said that these bonuses were all individual. He said that everyone got one, but they were different amounts. Divulging how much you received was a death sentence. Pretty harsh and not exactly fitting with workplace legislation but I understood why.

He slid the envelope across to me and then pushed a second one over. He said that I should count them both when I got to my room, explaining that there was one from him and one from his boss. He related the story about what happened and with millions of dollars in smack almost lost it really was a big deal. His boss was happy and looking forward to meeting me. I was both excited and worried at that comment. I hoped his boss was El Rey, but I also knew I would be in much deeper and the tiniest mistake could cost me my life.

Although Norie knew in general terms what was happening, Colin was my only real backup at this point. It was the most dangerous situation I had ever been in. When I was still in Special Force's I was virtually always undercover. In all but a few cases, nobody knew who I was until it was far too late to do anything about it. As I contemplated things, I marvelled that it was easier to take out a military foreign leader, billionaire international criminal or even a US senator than it was to get a drug lord like El Rey.

We had a glass of wine and I retired to my room. I was surprised when I opened the first envelope and found $10,000 but even more surprised when I opened the one from Arturo's boss and counted out $25,000. I knew the wounded warriors project would be thrilled to get $35,000. I was certain they would not like where it came from so I would continue to filter the money into them anonymously.

Various sums of cash mailed in or dropped off with some converted to money orders and other to prepaid Visa cards. I knew they would not accept cash acquired this way, but I also knew how much they needed it.

What followed was a couple of weeks of three or four of us driving to various meetings with Arturo and Javier. There were no more people getting killed or even threatened, that I saw. It seemed to be more of a show the face and build relationships kind of time. I suppose, when you got down to the short strokes, these guys were little more than high paid politicians. Protecting turf, ensuring loyalty, and buying off people.

There was one incident that caused me some concern. I had told Arturo long ago, and he agreed, that I would not fight for money or get into a cage or room again. I believed that I was now too valuable for him to think that. I suppose I may have gotten a little too comfortable.

This one seemed like another in a lengthy line of regular meetings, with underlings and partners paying homage to Arturo and, by connection, Arturo's boss. We did our usual sweep, positioned two of the boys outside the building with automatic weapons and went inside. Pablo was in front, followed by Javier and Arturo and I covered the rear. It was black tie, so I had both Berettas in my jacket and multiple clips. I even had a wasp knife hidden inside my boot.

We were all frisked, weapons placed on the table and then escorted into a dimly lit room with a few tables and chairs. It looked like some sort of poker room setup with an open area in the front. The open floor was maybe twelve feet by fourteen feet and the tables and chairs could seat twenty-four. I quickly surveyed the room and the people already inside.

Even with the dim lighting, you could see that it was a collection of criminals. We sat at a table near the front as others started to filter into the other tables. I had no idea what we were about to see but I initially thought I would have to sit there and watch strippers or something. Not like I hadn't had to do that before, but it didn't mean that I found it any less tasteless or not demeaning to women.

The objectification of women for the pleasure of these dirtbags disgusted me. That was when Arturo leaned over to me and whispered that he knows he had promised that I would not have to fight for pleasure or money again, but this was different.

He recounted the whole orchestra concept and said that this was another test. His boss knew what I had done, and he had said that he needed either me or Javier on his own team.

Javier was like a brother to him and as great as I was, he said that if his boss wanted me in his employ, he could not say no. People were killed for doing something as stupid as that. He smiled at me, looked into my eyes, and said this was my audition for first violin in the big orchestra!

Of course, this is exactly what I wanted so I tried to conceal my glee about this possible "promotion." I told him we agreed no more of this, but I also said I supposed this was different. I said that I would not want to see anything happen to him, so I would certainly do what he asked. I stood up, removed my jacket, and walked to the front of the room.

As I stood there, brighter lights shone on this area, and you could not see who was sitting at any of the tables. As my eyes became accustomed to the light, I saw a tall, Russian or Polish looking fellow stand. He removed his jacket and revealed powerful arms and chest encased in a tight black T shirt. He was obviously going to be a tough match for me. I surveyed his gait as he approached the floor and did not notice any potential weak areas.

The knee was still the knee but his were certainly surrounded by lots of muscle. Of course, with an accurate and powerful strike, the same muscles and ligaments that held a knee together could act like springs and blow it completely apart. I surmised that getting to his knees would be a challenging task.

As I looked him up and down, I knew I would have to use his own size and strength against him. I certainly could not go toe to toe with this one and I had no element of surprise acting in my favor either.

I also assumed that, while I knew nothing about him, that he had been told about me. Even so he still glared at me with a look of contempt as he evaluated me. Being a woman almost always aided me in these situations. All men seemed to be hardwired to think that they were somehow better and stronger than any woman. It made it easier to use their confidence against them. Often, they would expose themselves in ways they would never do if they were competing against a male.

I was never encumbered by such thoughts. Not about gender, race, or national origin. I had lived this long, doing what I was doing, because I assumed EVERY opponent, target, or even ally was completely capable of beating or killing me. It was this very concept that helped me do what I did. I was able to achieve a Zen-like sense of calmness in these situations because of that mindset.

I prepared myself as he stood glaring at me. The room was silent, nobody said anything. He reached out, offering his hand. I figured it was a trap so was prepared when he attempted to pull me hard into him and head butt me.

The guys from there just loved to use those rock-hard melons to try to blow somebody up early. I thought, in that second, that he may even be Albanian. It did not matter, I let him pull me in and thanks to me being shorter I only had to squat slightly to deliver an uppercut to his jaw with my own head. He rocked back but, much to my chagrin, did not seem very phased by the blow. He even smiled at me. Uh-oh!

I did not want this to go too long, and I knew that exchanging strikes was not my best choice. I would resort to Judo and Brazilian jiu-jitsu skills to start. He began to advance on me and as I was attempting to use his own arm as leverage, I felt a massive fist connect with my rib cage. He had serious power, even more than I thought, and his skill level appeared to be close to mine.

Mercifully, his massive fists spread the blow over multiple ribs. I knew immediately I would have a huge bruise and be tender for a week but at least he had not broken a rib. That could be fatal. As we danced around the small area attempting various strikes I noticed when he punched with his right hand, it was always to set up his left. I also saw that the blow with his right came straight out, the arm carried lower than his dominant left hand.

I knew then that I would use the Tobi Kubi-Kani Basami, a ninjutsu throw often seen attempted in the WWE.

Of course, it is much easier to accomplish when it is choreographed, and your "opponent" is playing along. That was not the case here. It was a high risk move but that was how you achieved great reward.

I watched and waited, absorbed, and deflected a few blows while hitting him with some good strikes. I could tell by his stance he was about to try the combination of punches, hoping he could knock me out. I prepared myself and when he threw the right I jumped, hooking his forearm under my leg. I grabbed his head and propelled myself up and onto his shoulders, simultaneously locking both legs around his neck.

My momentum took us both to the ground and I knew it would soon be over. I was locked in, still had a tight hold of one arm and he was losing consciousness. At almost the same time I broke his arm I felt a searing pain in my leg. I released him and rolled back to find a knife buried in my calf. So, weapons WERE in.

I extracted the knife as he groggily got to his feet. I tossed the knife away and as he moved in, I connected with a vicious kick to his groin, using my good leg. There was a lot of blood already and I knew this had to end quickly.

I snuck my own knife from its hiding place in my boot and concealed it with my hand. The wasp knife did not need a long blade, so it was easy to hide. I might have to absorb a hard strike, but I knew that I wanted to bury that knife between his ribs. I would only require a split second to get the knife in, hit the button and watch him explode.

I kept the knife hidden my hand low against my body. He knew he had hurt me with the shot to the ribs so that was a great cover. He would think I was protecting my ribs from further damage and that he had the edge. Combined with the stab wound and blood running down my leg I felt certain he would come in for the kill.

Sure enough, he did. He led with his strong hand and connected with my face as I buried the knife in his chest cavity. He hit me hard, and I was down and almost out. I awoke on my back on the floor, my head killing me and likely a broken jaw, but I was looking into Javier's eyes. "You did it, you did it," he yelled at me.

He helped me up and into a chair and that was when I noticed the blood and guts everywhere. The tiny floor looked like a war zone. They said they both thought I was a goner and then watched as the other guy's side exploded outward. They said he went down in a heap and still had a stunned look on his face.

The room was empty except for a tiny bespectacled gentleman who said he was a doctor, and he would fix me up. I sat there as he disinfected the wound and bandaged it like a pro. He patched up some of the other cuts and then gently manipulated my jaw, exclaiming it was not broken.

Then he just got up and left. The room was empty except for us. Javier and Pablo helped me back to the SUV. I was a little woozy as that guy packed a real punch. As we drove back to the compound Arturo said he would be terribly sad to see me go but this was how their organization worked. They never had a choice. I looked at him and asked who my new boss would be.

He said his name was Alejandro, Alejandro Flores Garcia.

I maintained a stoic look and asked if he was at least a good guy. Did Alejandro treat his people as well as I had been treated here. He said that he did but also stressed that any mistake or slight could resort in death. He went on to share that, after what I did today, that he would value me very highly. I had just bested a man who had been his main protector for more than seven years. Alejandro realized the value of having someone like me at his side.

He told me I would soon be living either in Los Mochis or Loreto, both of which were in Mexico. Obviously, I knew the area well, but I asked some basic questions to display that I did not. I asked when I would go there, and he said it would happen on the boats. We would meet, I would bring all personal possessions with me and that would be that.

I knew, without a doubt I would be searched so I would need to sanitize my room. That would include getting my various electronic devices to Colin and getting rid of some of my bonus money. I was surprised I was given any advance warning, but I had two days to clear out.

I thanked him for the opportunity and when we returned to the compound, I sent a message to Colin using the other wireless network. I just said gym. I had a secret compartment inside my gym bag, so I retrieved all my devices and stashed them inside. I threw in my shoes, lifting straps and belt and the smelliest gym shirt I could find to top it off.

I awoke the next day and said I wanted to get in a final workout. I was surprised I was allowed to go. For the first time in a long while I noticed I was being followed. It was a silver four door Audi. I thought I had seen it before but not in our compound. In California, those things were all over the place though, so it could have been anyone. I took a circuitous route to the gym and confirmed they were indeed following me. I could see there were two guys in the front, no idea if there were more in the back.

I assumed, now that I was his, that they worked for El Rey. Of course, they may have been buddies with the guy I had killed in that room and perhaps they were going to exact revenge. One could never be certain of what was motivating these people.

I arrived at the gym, changed, and got ready for my workout. I had a large, opaque water bottle and stashed the electronics and some cash inside and I went out to train. I wasn't in the mood for a run but wouldn't have gone for one anyway, so I just got lifting. I had to keep it lighter than usual as I was still tender in a few spots from my "audition." I pretended to drink from my water bottle as I lifted until Colin arrived.

He had the same bottle and we switched where nobody could see. I had written a brief note telling him of my promotion, where I was going and the timeline. We did not acknowledge each other or have any conversation. We could always be under surveillance, so no chances could be taken. At least he would know where I was headed and could hopefully get close.

Chapter 30 One – The Spoils Of Crime & My New Boss

The day came to set sail and I was surprised the boys had a little going away party for me. The feelings seemed mixed. Some appeared happy to see me moving on up and others expressed fear for me. They explained that I shouldn't be fooled by Alejandro's polite manners and charm. He was called El Rey De Los Muertos for a reason.

Javier toasted me with yet another bottle of fine wine and asked if I was happy to be moving. I said I would miss these guys but would always remember them. Arturo piped up and said that he hoped I would have many, many years to remember.

Here I was at a typical office-type, going away party with a bunch of criminals, killers, and drug lords. It was surreal on a number of fronts. The sad thing was we were not THAT odd of bedfellows. If I'm being honest, these days, I probably fit in better with these people than most others. I knew I would not be seeing all my friends for quite a while. Jonathon and Kathy, Luke, and Angela, Norie, they would all need to be kept at maximum distance.

As evening approached my bags were all carried out to the car and Javier, Arturo and I went down to the boat.

The crew was already preparing and there were two other security guys already on board. It was a pleasant evening, as they most always were here, and we got underway in short order.

We were going to meet in the ocean, further South of our location.

Alejandro and his people would be waiting for us, enjoying a little fishing time while they waited. We sailed out and then headed South. The winds were in our favor, and we were travelling at a good clip. I watched as the bow gently broke through the waves, barely noticing any up and down motion on the boat itself. The crew must be a good one.

I could tell we were quite a way South and had entered Mexican waters, travelling within view of the Baja peninsula. I figured we would not go too far South but, based on landmarks, I felt we were close to being across the peninsula from Loreto. That was when I spotted the boat.

The Ngoni was even more impressive in daylight than it was at night. I kept an eye on it as we got closer and closer, the boat (or should I say ship) seeming to grow in length and height as we closed the distance. It was an imposing craft to be sure. I had never seen anything like it, and it appeared completely different in daylight than it did in the dark.

It is difficult to paint an accurate picture. It appeared very sleek and extremely fast, even when moving slowly through the waves. The shape, design, and curves of it were like a much smaller, racing boat than a luxury yacht. The gleaming hull seemed to pierce the waves and be unaffected by the four-foot swells.

It just kept moving smoothly towards us, sails already dropped. Its large mainsail already furrowed into the massive housing that held it. There were no bumpers being deployed this time. They would send over a small landing craft, and I would be ferried over that way. Too dangerous to have the authorities see two massive craft moored together here.

Once we were both static and sitting a little less than half a mile apart, I saw the deck open on the Ngoni and a crane lift a zodiac style boat out of its belly. It was lowered slowly over the side and was moored to Arturo's boat in seconds it seemed.

As I looked over the starboard side of our boat I could see why. It was a zodiac style but more like those Coast Guard boats I had seen. Two, 250 HP outboards anchored to the back of it meant it could likely travel at 60 mph, maybe even seventy. I shook hands with Javier and was surprised when Arturo hugged me. He thanked me for saving him and being such a good soldier.

They threw my bags down to the waiting boat while I climbed down the ladder they had tossed over the side. There was only one man in the boat, and he said nothing as he untied us and then gunned it back to his own boat. I was shocked when we went around to the port side of the craft to see a stairwell sticking out the side, complete with its own platform. Swim ladder and everything!

The guy tied us up and then I hopped out onto the platform and walked up nine steps to the deck. I stepped off the top step onto the perfectly clean and smooth deck, steadying myself by holding the stainless-steel railing. I was overwhelmed by what I saw. Arturo's boat was amazing, but this thing was out of this world.

I first saw the curved cabin with half its glass opened and half closed.

Everything was smooth and sleek with compound curving angles everywhere. I looked straight ahead at two different control seats, one on each side of the craft. I suppose due its size and the fact you sailed it that was a requirement. I looked to the left and sunken into the deck was a large hot tub.

As I got my bearings an attractive man came to me and extended his hand. As he shook my hand he said, "welcome to my home away from home."

He waved an arm around in a sweeping gesture and said, "this is why I do what I do. I am Alejandro." I smiled and said he could call me Meg. He handed me off almost immediately to one of his men who took me around the topsides first. It was amazing. A long row of curved steps off the stern led to another set of stairs and a swim platform.

We went inside and before going below I was shown the lounge and one of the dining areas. There was even a bar with stools for eight people and a curved, quartz-like countertop with a well-stocked bar behind it. We then went down more stairs to the guest section below deck. It looked like the most expensive of hotel rooms. Gleaming teak, stainless steel, and stonework everywhere.

I was shown a room, with twin beds, which would be mine when I was on board. It was right out front of what I was told was El Rey's stateroom.

We went back up on deck and then descended a separate set of stairs that led to control rooms and crew quarters along with the galley. The galley was like nothing I had ever seen, shiny stainless steel everywhere. Large commercial freezer and fridge and room for the crew to eat right there.

Large specially equipped gas cooktops and multiple ovens meant you could easily cook for twenty. It truly was stunning.

We went back top-side and Alejandro apologized for being pulled away. He said we should sit at the back and discuss a few things.

He walked ahead of me as he spoke, and we sat in two chairs looking out the stern. He explained that his job was not easy, nor would mine be easy. Today was likely the first and only time I would enjoy a day of relaxation.

He explained that many people were after him and, even with friends in extremely high places, his life was always in danger. It was my job to ensure he was safe. He explained that Artan had done that for him for seven years. He had seen Artan take a bullet for him and endure brutal beatings to save his boss. That was now my job.

He went on to say that he had never expected anyone, ever, to best Artan. The Albanians had a tolerance for pain that others seemed to lack. He had watched many challengers attempt to unseat him and none had come even remotely close to doing so. He hoped that I would be up to my new task. I said that I would, and he would learn that.

The whole time he was speaking I maintained eye contact. He was, indeed, a very eloquent and soft-spoken man. He had deep brown eyes and hints of grey in his black hair. I estimated him to be, maybe fifty years of age. He was almost too attractive to be doing what he was doing. He sort-of resembled that Esai Morales actor from TV and movies. Even though Morales was of Puerto Rican descent they could almost be brothers.

I could not let his good looks, demeanor, eloquence, perfect smile, and all-around good boy looks confuse me. This man was a cold-blooded killer and those around him were all killers too. He was the leader of the Mochismo cartel and came by the moniker El Rey De Los Muertos quite honestly. He had killed many men, although none the way that I had. He exclusively used guns to carry out his will or used those around him to do his dirty work. As pretty as he was, I thought it highly unlikely he had even thrown a punch since grade school, if even then.

He told me a little more about the organization and the people but kept it all very superficial. Finally, he shared that we were on our way to our home base in Los Mochis. I let him tell me about the area as if I knew little of it. He told me of large, tree lined streets and the Sinaloa cartel amongst others. He seemed quite proud of El Chepe, the only passenger train in Mexico.

Its real name is the Chihuahua-Pacific railway but even the cars themselves proudly display El Chepe on the sides in bold, bright letters. As one might assume it runs between Chihuahua and Los Mochis on the coast, traversing the copper canyon.

On either side are the Sonora and Durango regions of Mexico. Once at the coast you are in Sinaloa. El Chepe is popular with tourists from all over the world. Basically, it's Mexican Amtrak.

Seemingly in no time, we were rounding the tip of the peninsula and passing Cabo San Lucas as we headed up the Gulf of California.

You could see Mazatlán on one side of the inlet and Cabo on the other. Yup, this was party-central in Mexico for adults and college kids alike.

We were moving more slowly, and I heard the engines start up to add to the sail power. Soon the sails were dropped completely, and we continued our trek North under power. I watched out the starboard side as we slowly moved past the main port, Topolobampo. Soon we were easing into a large slip at what appeared to be a private deep-water dock. There were built in bumpers but there was also a system of ropes and pulleys that kept the hull of this behemoth safely away from anything solid anyway.

The crew got us all locked up and I followed El Rey and his men to the parked vehicles. More FBI-style mafia staff cars were waiting. They looked like they were prepared the same way and built by the same people who built Arturo's SUV. There were three identical vehicles and we got into the middle one. I could tell it was indeed the same vehicle as Arturo's. It looked and felt the same and I was confident it had all the same "options."

Los Mochis was further inland than I recalled but soon we rolled up on the compound. It was between the city and the coastline, pretty much in the middle of the desert. He explained the compound was impenetrable.

The walls were constructed of sixteen inches of high strength concrete with three-inch steel plate in the middle. The roof was similar.

He was quite proud to tour me around and show me the various areas and even the bomb shelter type bunker that comprised pretty much what would have been a basement. Except for the fact it was more than twenty feet below the surface and safe from virtually any attack. I knew there must be an escape tunnel or tunnels from there but thought it better not to ask. He got one of his guys to show me to my room and I was pleasantly surprised.

It appeared being the number one protector of El Rey had its benefits. My room was right out front of his, just like on the boat. Of course, the downside of the accommodations was it would make it extremely difficult to get any electronics inside. I would also be likely unable to meet or communicate with Colin, but that would remain to be seen. There was a large gym on site, a gun range and everything else anyone might want or need.

I was on my own. I felt confident Colin would eventually find his way down here but a backup of one wouldn't help much with this crowd.

They were safely ensconced in a bomb-proof and attack-proof compound with a small army to protect it. There was also the highly likely scenario that the "people in high places" stretched to the pinnacle of the Mexican government, and likely similar connections in the USA.

This was not going to be easy, and I calculated a fifty-fifty chance that I could escape alive and return to my comfy California, surfer-dude life.

Chapter 30 Two - The Mochismo Life

I settled in surprisingly easily. I expected pushback from at least some of the men but it never came. I supposed that, because I had killed Artan instead of just beating him, there was an element of fear mixed in with respect. I did not care one bit whether I was feared or respected as long as none of them screwed with me. If so, I would just beat them within an inch of their miserable life and go about my business.

I was next introduced to Diego who was going to show me the ropes for the next couple of days. The first thing we did was spend a couple of hours reviewing and scouting out the access points to various parts of the compound. I had a retinal scan as well which, along with a numerical code, was the only way to get in or out of the various areas and control points. Once that was all setup we continued our tour, using my scan and code to make sure everything worked.

Once we completed that part of the tour, we went to the motor garage to take a closer look at the SUV's. Diego said they were all exactly the same and that whenever El Rey was travelling all three were to be used. He never rode in the same one, and all the windows were blacked out, so nobody knew which one carried him. Just like the President.

They may be able to withstand an RPG attack or an IED, but they were not indestructible. Each was equipped with a sophisticated GPS system that also listed the locations of all the hiding vaults between Los Mochis and the coast. For the most part these safe rooms were a series of unconnected concrete sewer vaults, buried deep underground.

They were used in case of emergency and were undetectable from the surface. Basically, if you were unable to avoid pursuit or attack, the GPS would lead you to the closest vault. They were all in indentations in the landscape so that one could be bouncing along through the hills and the people following you would lose visual every now and then. During a loss you would stop, quickly drop into the vault, and then send the vehicle on alone.

They were programmed to continue on a pre-determined course for three miles away from the vault and then simply shut down. When they did shut down, after such a situation, all memory was instantly erased from the GPS. It was a serious defense system. If I had access to all my equipment, I was certain I could have used that same system to carry out my plan. But I did not so there was no sense in whining about it.

It amazed me as I learned more about the compound, the vehicles, and the boats. I suppose money could certainly buy a lot of things and perhaps even a certain amount of happiness.

It could not guarantee 100% safety. I was living proof of that fact. We finished the tour for the day and soon it was time for dinner.

I went and got cleaned up and then returned to the dining room. It was a separate building within the compound, large and ornate.

It was clearly designed to impress anyone who saw it. There was a massive table with a huge, candelabra centred over it. It hung from a deep, rough textured beam that traversed the entire room. That central candelabra must have been there for years and years.

The wax stretched all the way to the table like dangling tentacles from each candle. One row dripping down to the next and that row to the one below it until it finally cascaded down to the table where it pooled. It was quite amazing to see. The long table was hewn from multiple trees judging by the grain. I had no idea what type of wood, but I was later told it was made from Mexican Teak. It was inlaid with various pieces of copper and the chairs were all made of copper and the same wood, padded, and covered with well-worn leather.

The table was exceptionally long with ten chairs down each side and one larger armchair at one end. There was a well-established seating plan and when I entered, Diego pointed at the seat to El Rey's left. His right-hand man was just there, at his right side.

I was the protector from all else, including that right hand man. He was another dangerous looking man, although he appeared Mexican, unlike Artan.

He had a darker complexion and a ponytail. He was another guy with a huge set of arms and a menacing look on his face. He glared across at me, knowing what my purpose was, and reinforcing his own status in case I was unaware.

Alejandro looked at each of us and just said Megan meet Mateo. Get to know each other as we will be together often. Frequently in these cartels, it was usually the second highest man who attempted a coup. The seating plan was no fluke. I had direct, unobstructed aim at the right-hand man at all times. Mine was a position requiring constant vigilance so, unbeknownst to them, they could not have picked anyone better.

I watched as servers dispensed wine from a massive hogshead against the wall into large decanters. There were eight of them lined up in racks. Each hogshead is the equivalent of two barrels, holding roughly three hundred bottles of wine equivalent. That is a LOT of vino. Once every glass was full, El Rey stood and raised his glass to continued success. He highlighted that this was a new cask, imported directly from Spain.

It was a Rioja, made from Tempranillo grapes and was one of his favorites. He had tasted it a couple of years earlier and immediately bought two hogsheads. He shared that it was an Artadi , Vina El Pison, Rioja. Although it was only a 2012 vintage it tasted like it had been aged for decades. Its smoothness and finish rewarded with top marks by many wine critics. It came from a tiny vineyard, only 2.4 hectares in size and was highly regarded as one of Spain's best wines. I couldn't help but smile at Alejandro, a real renaissance man it seemed.

As we had a new team member, he thought a new cask would be appropriate. He looked at each person around the table as he slowly said, " Wine moistens and tempers the spirit and lulls the cares of the mind to rest. It revives our joys and is oil to the dying flame of life." Everyone drank as he sat down. It truly was an amazing tasting wine. My throat warmed as the ruby-red liquid slid down, leaving behind an aftertaste that almost overwhelmed my taste buds. Not that I was an oenophile or anything, but I had developed some taste and knowledge. I knew this too, was a delicious wine.

I would later find out that one bottle of this sold for over $475.00 USD! That means each of those massive wooden casks was worth close to $150,000! I knew the drug business paid well. I also found out that the two casks were transported over on the Ngoni.

It was a most amazing lifestyle, when you weren't being shot at, poisoned, or worrying your own people might try to kill you. And that is without factoring in the various law enforcement agencies working to eradicate the drug problem in the Americas.

With all that in mind I supposed that it made sense to relax and party and enjoy the trip. Much like my Special Forces compadres, other Navy SEALs and others serving their country, there was the ever-present chance of death. Everyone comes to accept that in their own way and deal with it in their own way. Most of us develop a somewhat warped sense of humor, able to make fun of even the worst situation. It is one way to maintain your sanity.

In my case, I chose to believe that I was already well past my expiry date. There had been so many times when I should have died and, almost died. I sometimes felt I had no business still walking this earth. That gave me a calmness that I used to keep my thoughts and emotions straight at the worst of times. It enabled me to weather torture while I waited for an opportunity to strike when others would have simply given up.

It helped me maintain an acute focus on the task at hand and execute whichever plan I had designed.

Everyone complimented Alejandro on the wine, and we feasted and drank, although not to excess.

He turned towards me and asked if I really did like the wine. I just said it was utterly amazing. He was a captivating speaker and obviously a charismatic leader. I had to remind myself what a disgusting killer he was as I looked into his dark, brooding eyes. If I weren't who I was, and he wasn't who he was, I think we could have been quite the power couple.

I would need to watch out for that charm. I needed to stay on my guard, drink little, and ensure that I did not put myself in an unsafe position. This was an extremely dangerous man, as were his competitors.

Everything started to wrap up and I said I needed to get some sleep. Would it be all right if I excused myself? He laughed and said he was not my father. I could do as I wished when I wished. Something felt odd when he said it. I couldn't put my finger on it, I was just left with an uneasy feeling. I wandered off to my room, locked the door and got into shorts and a tank top. The air conditioning worked very well but they kept it quite warm anyway.

I heard a knock on my door, and it was Diego. He said we had a job to do tomorrow, and I should be ready to leave by 7:00 AM. He said it was black tie and we were going out on the boat.

I was ready and waiting the next morning a few minutes before 7:00 in the entry when I was joined by Diego and two others. We took two of the large SUV's and began driving.

I assumed we were headed to the sailboat, but we did not go there.

Instead, we veered a slightly different direction when we got close to a different dock. We all boarded a large power yacht. It looked like a converted fishing boat or something similar.

Parked on the other side of the slip was one of those Mystic speedboats, like I had seen at Arturo's marina. I was secretly glad we were not taking that thing, after what the guy in La Jolla had told me about it. I heard the large engines power up on our boat and soon we were motoring down the peninsula at a fairly good clip. Diego said we were picking up some people. They were not expecting any trouble, but we always must be prepared. If enemies cannot get to El Rey, getting to his people was always an effective way to damage the organization.

I had no idea how long we travelled down the Coast. I wasn't sure where we were, but soon we pulled into a well disguised boat slip. We docked, tied ourselves off and waited. What used to be the fish hold was outfitted with a second room, lined with chairs.

At first, I thought we were smuggling illegal immigrants but then I saw the girls. They were clearly handcuffed, scantily clothed and all quite pretty.

They appeared to be South American, and I shuddered when I knew what they were headed into. Twelve girls were ushered aboard, all looked to be between fifteen and maybe twenty.

One of the guys carefully helped them down into the hold, they were all seat-belted in and the separating door was closed. Soon we were back underway, and Diego could tell I was concerned. What I was, was mad!

I wanted to shoot all three of them, release all the girls and then head back saying we were ambushed. I knew that would help nobody though, so I was stuck. I did my best to keep my feelings inside and not let my disgust drive me to do something stupid.

Diego said "we" were not only about drugs. Alejandro believed in diversifying his income streams. There were car businesses, brothels, drugs of course, liquor, building supplies and girls. He explained that each of these girls represented more than $250,000/year if employed in their brothels. In this load there were even two virgins. Diego said they would likely bring $100,000 or $200,000 each if sold. El Rey may choose to keep one himself, you never knew.

These girls were all extremely attractive and it sickened me when I thought what was going to happen to them.

I was really struggling with what could be done. If I exterminated the three guys on the way back, I would have no explanation for where the girls went. And, if I did release them, I would be worried the story of what happened would make its way back to El Rey. I could not take the chance. It appeared that, at this moment, I had no choice but to continue. This little trip may accelerate the execution of my plan though. I knew I could not sit by and let this happen.

It was a quiet trip back for me. I did my best to keep some distance between me and the guys by wandering around on the deck. They said there was nothing to be nervous about and I told them I was just in need of a workout and maybe some shooting practice. They all agreed that was a great idea and we could use the range when we got back.

It what seemed like too short a time we were back at our dock. We put six of the girls into each vehicle and went directly to the compound. I was beside myself as I drove back, wanting to roll the vehicle or something. For the first time in an awfully long time, I felt powerless. There was nothing I could do right now to help these women. I would have to get information to Colin somehow or take care of things myself once El Rey was gone.

Soon the gates opened, and we rolled into the middle of the compound.

I parked the SUV I was driving and watched as two girls were segregated from the others and taken to an upstairs room. The remaining ten were led into a larger building. Afterwards, as I was walking to the range, I saw a couple of groups of happy looking guys walking into the same building. I tried to block out of my mind what was happening in there.

I put in my ear plugs and headphone protection and set my Beretta Tomcats down on the counter in front of me. I went to the back wall to grab ammunition, a couple of nine mms, and a .223 calibre automatic weapon. I set the targets twenty-five yards out and grabbed a Tomcat in each hand. There were a couple of the boys watching me as I unloaded a full clip from each pistol into the two targets. I reeled them in and confirmed I had shot the lights out with only three bullets outside the center circles.

I got two more targets, clipped them on and sent them out twenty-five yards. The nine-millimetre pistols were Sig Sauer's, older models known as P210's. It is still considered one of the most accurate pistols ever made. The P210 was the forerunner of all the "P" series pistols that came after it once Sauer got involved. The SIG (Swiss) company was founded in 1853 with Sauer (German) partnering with them in 1976.

Unlike many of today's sidearms the P210 has only an eight-shot clip rather than the 10 and 15's favored by Glock. It was extremely popular as a target pistol due to its five-inch barrel and 3.5-pound trigger pull.

I loaded the clips and took my stance, starting with my right hand. I reeled off eight shots in quick succession and then took the other pistol and did the same with my left hand. Firing accuracy with a nine mil is best using a staggered, two-handed grip and that is what I did.

Once I unclipped and cleared both weapons the guys came to my lane as I rolled in the target. The center circle was all but obliterated by the sixteen shots, all of which would have been center-mass on a body. We slipped off our hearing protection and they both said nice shooting, for a girl.

We all laughed because I knew they all well aware I could easily crush them in a competition seeing what I had just done. They would have also known what I had done to Artan, so I'm certain that would be front of mind for them. They wanted to look at my Tomcats, so I handed them each one and they said they were so light and small. I highlighted that was the whole point of them, easy to conceal with a tiny 2 ½ inch barrel but a .32 calibre slug would still do a lot of damage, especially up close.

They nodded their agreement and asked how I did shooting single-handed.

I suppose they had not paid close attention when I was shooting the tomcats. I loaded another target and sent it out twenty-five yards. I slipped a new clip into one of the P210's and stood at 90 degrees to the target. I had one hand fully extended toward the target and fired off all eight shots. One guy whistled when I reeled it in and had put all eight in the inner circle.

I highlighted the advantage of doing that was the target presented to your attacker was one third the width of a two-footed stance. They nodded their approval.

I didn't bother shooting the assault rifle. It wasn't like I really needed practice anyway, I was just blowing off steam. As I left the range, I smiled as I watched them practicing single hand shooting with their own nine mil's. Lots of misses! That was good to know, not that I was worried about these imbeciles anyway.

I wanted to get back to my room and see if there wasn't something I could do to help these girls. I could not simply stand by and do nothing.

It was unlikely I could help the two innocent ones but there may be something I could do for the others. Their fate would be close to top of mind for me until they were free.

Chapter 30 Three – Delivery Of The Girls

A couple of days later Diego told me that he would need me to accompany him and one other guy to Los Mochis. We were going to make a delivery and he needed backup. Of course, I said I would be happy to help. I figured we would be delivering drugs.

A large white van pulled into the compound as we were getting ready. It looked like one of those airporter vans with about sixteen seats or so. The guy honked the horn and Diego, and I went out to the door of the van. The other fellow who was coming with us then led the ten girls out of the building they had been housed in. All looked to have been cleaned up, made up, dressed up and ready to go.

I knew we were taking this group to one of the brothels and I immediately began reviewing scenarios in my head. I looked at each girl as they got dejectedly into the van, clearly knowing what was ahead for them. They looked even younger than I originally thought, and I nearly puked right then and there.

Finally, everyone was loaded, and we drove slowly out of the compound. Diego and the other guy were in the two front seats, and I was in the very last row by myself.

They said there was almost never a problem making these deliveries but every now and then a competing cartel might try to ambush them and take the girls.

I quickly began to think through a plan. I would not have much time as anything that was going to happen would have to happen before we got too close to Los Mochis. I knew the driver was one of our men and they would all be well armed. I had both my Tomcats and six full clips, so they wouldn't know what hit them. I decided on a plan and waited until we seemed to be in the most secluded location.

I knew that whatever I did, I would need to hurt myself too. The girls could know nothing. Once the three guys were shot and I was incapacitated, they could take off in the van and head South or to the authorities. I was sure one of them would know what to do. It was risky and dangerous, but I was not about to watch these poor girls get beaten and drugged into a life of unpaid prostitution.

We were likely about six miles away from the compound, there were no vehicles anywhere and we were coming up on some abandoned buildings. I knew it was now or never. I had one arm out the window and fired a couple of shots up towards the front tire and windows.

I was hoping that, even though the angle was steep, that the window might shatter, and it did. I quickly pulled my arm in and yelled at all the girls to get their heads down and stay on the floor. I moved to the front of the van and crouched in the door well. I said I saw more up ahead, and we should probably move cross country. The driver turned off onto the sand and gunned it.

That was when I took my shot at getting freedom for these girls. I slipped a Tomcat into each hand and shot Diego and the other guy.

Before the driver could get his weapon, I put one right between his eyes. Thankfully, he fell inward so his foot came off the gas pedal. As we began to slow, I opened the door and rolled out onto the sand. I shot myself on the side of my stomach where I knew the bullet would go through and through. I also knew there were no organs and that I could control the bleeding long enough to get me back to camp. I then took one of my pistols and hit myself as hard as I could on the side of my face.

I came around a few minutes later with a splitting headache, cursing myself for wanting to make this so convincing. I could feel blood oozing from a cut and running slowly down my face. I watched as the van was about to disappear in the distance. I was sure they would have thrown the bodies out. The advantage of doing what I had done was that it would appear someone entered the front and shot them. When we left the compound, I was the only one in the rear so could say I escaped that way. I felt the story would work.

I felt a little bad about shooting Diego but not too much. These guys were all the scum of the earth, and I had no doubt that he too had participated in "partying" with those girls back in the compound.

Thankfully, it was early in the day and the weather was not as hot as it could have been. I tore my shirt into strips and wrapped my stomach to stem the bleeding. I knew there was no issue with organs or a bullet inside me, so I was quite confident I would be fine.

I took the rest of the shirt and fashioned a hat to keep the sun off my head and began walking towards the road.

I had been sipping on a bottle of water, so I had that with me too. I just hoped that I could get back to the compound before anyone drove down that road. It would be more convincing if I staggered in and passed out rather than got a ride.

The day quickly got much hotter than I had hoped as I walked the six or so miles back. I wondered if I hadn't overextended myself and wished I had a measly six-mile swim ahead of me instead. I walked at a reasonable pace with only a couple of cars passing me heading towards Los Mochis. They didn't stop or even give me a second glance.

Finally, lips cracked, and dry and water bottle long empty I staggered up to the control gate at the compound. I looked into the scanner and then punched in my code and the gate swung slowly open. I staggered and fell as the gate closed behind me and two of the guys came running up to me asking what happened. They each grabbed an arm and got me out of the sun.

I told them we had been ambushed. All three men were dead, and I had escaped out the rear door. I know I shot one of them but then I got shot and pistol whipped. I told them I was out cold, and they probably thought I was dead. Thankfully, nobody questioned why they did not pump a couple of shots into my head. They got me water and more people showed up as I told and retold my story.

Then Alejandro was walking toward me with his right-hand goon.

I was on edge as, even with my skills, if something were to happen now there was no way I was getting out alive. I laid out my story for both of them and Alejandro was asking if I saw anything, did I recognize anyone? Any vehicles? In a case like this the best option is to keep the story as simply as possible. Superfluous details added in hopes of making the story more believable typically had the opposite effect. Plus, those very details were the ones you could easily forget.

I stuck to a clear and concise ambush story. The van stopped because there was a couple of old people blocking the road. I heard the shots soon after the front door opened. I returned fire and then used the back door to get out. That was when I got shot and hit. He seemed quite convinced but must have had some concerns. After all, I had demolished Artan, and he knew that I had also taken out two trained killers at the same time in that ring. I seemed okay, for now, but certainly could not let any complacency worm its way into my head.

I went to a room they called the infirmary where an older, little doctor patched me up. He gave me some antibiotics and I was out of there. There was lots to do, but I was told to rest for a few days so that I was 100% ready to work.

They had no idea that the work I was going to undertake would mean their boss's demise.

Chapter 30 Four – R&R In The Compound

I went to my room passed and out on the bed. It was a lot cooler than outside, and the coolness felt good on my hot, clammy skin. I would shower the next day I decided. I popped a couple of the antibiotics and what I figured were Tylenol 3's and pretty much passed out immediately.

I awoke in the morning feeling better than I expected. It's not like I hadn't been shot before or pistol-whipped before, for that matter. I had a high tolerance for pain. I decided I would use this R&R time to produce a plan.

Thanks to our exchange at the gym, Colin knew where I was going. I would have preferred some sort of electronics with me but we both felt it was much too dangerous with these guys. Get caught with a personal cell or other device and you would likely soon be "swimming with the fishes" as the mafioso liked to say. I was confident that Colin would, at a minimum get to Los Mochis, and then locate me here. Man, oh man, did I ever appreciate all the tech I had access to before. I was now, for the most part, completely on my own.

At least I had saved those girls, but I had no idea about the other two. Was El Rey keeping them for himself or perhaps planning to make them a gift to one of his largest customers or suppliers?

I had no idea, but I hoped for the latter, as that would give me a shot at saving them before such a dastardly act. It really wasn't too bad being in that compound while convalescing. Whatever business there was, it was going on without me and within a few days I was back in action. I was at the range every day and got back to training again too.

It wasn't a big deal for me, but I think it added to my mystique when I was shooting, lifting, and sparring after being shot only five days earlier. They must have thought I was part Superwoman or something. I chuckled to myself as I considered that I WAS part Superwoman, at least when compared to these clowns. Mateo was the only one that really worried me, but I had my methods for taking down guys his size.

Each night everyone got together in the dining hall for a big meal and while the wine did not flow like water there was always wine at the table. Everyone seemed to understand it was a one glass with dinner thing, these guys weren't pirates after all. As I sat across from Mateo, I could tell he was still wary of me. It was just a feeling I had, and I knew I would need to be careful. As good as I was, he appeared like he would be a formidable opponent.

I had a few more recovery days under my belt when Mateo approached me in the yard.

There was an annual celebration in Los Mochis this weekend and Alejandro never missed the event. As Los Mochis was a major commercial center for the large agricultural area in the basin of the El Fuerte river, they had an annual harvest festival. People came from all over for a weekend of fun, eating and drinking. It sounded like drinking was number one with eating being a close second.

I had a vague recollection of the festival from when I was last in the area.

As Los Mochis is positioned on the border between Sinaloa and Sonora that meant there were numerous cartel people who would attend. From what Mateo told me it was an opportunity to fly the flag and even take out the odd enemy. Quietly and behind the scenes of course, so as not to disturb the fun. He said that El Rey found it a most opportune time to further demonstrate his power and influence. Weaker rivals could pay homage to the powerful El Rey and he would make it a point to be seen with many high-ranking government officials and chiefs of police.

I would come to learn that Alejandro held degrees from the Universidad Autonoma de Occidente, its main campus was in Los Mochis. Many of his relationships were forged while attending that university. I believed that there were likely those who, even though they were in positions of power in law enforcement and government, remained fearful of one Alejandro Flores Garcia.

I was also confident there were others on which he likely had career-ending, if not life-ending, dirt, and scandals with which to guarantee their cooperation or ignorance. I wondered what the school, whose motto is "For The Culture of Liberty" would think about the lifestyle of one of their most infamous sons?

Speaking of liberty, Los Mochis was also the place where El Chapo lost his liberty, for a second time. He was recaptured on January

8th of 2016. President Nieto was beside himself as he announced, "Mission accomplished: We have him." He seemed proud to tell Mexico and the world that Joaquin Archivaldo Guzman Loera was in captivity once more.

I wondered if El Chapo had simply stopped paying off the people he needed to pay off or if this really was the government and law enforcement doing their job? In Mexico, one was just never quite sure.

Turned out one of the main reasons El Chapo was recaptured was his own vanity. He was keen to make a film about himself. He and his representatives were working with producers and actors. This created an opening for deeper investigation and surveillance that would help pinpoint his whereabouts. Similar vanity had brought about the demise of others, but most were still on the run from the law.

Alejandro seemed to be bullet-proof and Teflon-coated. There were no outstanding charges on him.

In fact he had never been successfully convicted of anything. Witnesses frequently disappeared, stories rapidly changed and ultimately nobody would stand up to him. That would be a jury on which even I would hate to sit.

With El Chapo back behind bars and the Sinaloa cartel in disarray, El Rey de Los Muertos was the king of kings. At least for the moment.

Chapter 30 Five – Fiesta de la Cosecha

The Harvest Festival was a huge gathering of all kinds of people. The city and the government would like one to believe this harvest celebrates the agricultural area surrounding Los Mochis. In fact, there was a much larger, at least on a dollar basis, harvest. With fertile land and access to water, combined with lots of sun and warm temperatures, it was also about growing the plants that provide the feedstock for illegal drugs.

I knew the festival would be a dangerous time to attempt this, but I also knew it would be the easiest for me to cover up. While I would prefer the painful death of an air embolus injected into his vein, I would most likely use a garotte on Alejandro. It would be very believable that a rival cartel would kill him that way. He was a fan of the weapon plus it was quick and relatively clean. The variables would include Mateo and if there was any opportunity for me to get him alone at some point. Security for him and the other cartel leaders would be very heavy. It would be difficult, but not impossible to complete my task and get away.

We were all briefed about where we would go and who Alejandro wanted to see. We would arrive close to noon with El Rey visiting some people he knew, sharing a drink, and then leaving.

By 6:00 PM we would be at Pitahaya Costes, one of Alejandro's favorite spots. He loved the food and the whole restaurant was booked solely for our group and a few invited guests.

Soon we were loading ourselves into the three SUV's and heading to the center of the city. We stopped at least five times. Each time we stopped the vehicles two men got out of each of the other two SUV's, automatic weapons (Mac 10's I assumed) hanging from straps beneath their jackets. They would scan the rooftops and street and one would approach the door of the house or building. Once it was opened then El Rey would exit the vehicle, me on one side and Mateo on the other. It was like the secret service guarding the President.

The first time we exited the vehicle, I noticed that Alejandro was wearing a special vest with his dark suit. Based on the way the vest hung and its size I knew it was armor plated. I suppose when you were one of these guys there was no sense taking chances. Of course, all the armor plate in the world wasn't going to protect his throat from me.

Finally, we drove up and parked all three vehicles on the street in front of the outdoor patio at Pitahaya Costes. The patio ran the full length of the restaurant, and the three SUVs pretty much blocked the whole thing. Being bulletproof and practically bomb-proof they made a good shield. The only issue was they also completely blocked the sightlines from inside.

As we walked in, I noted that one heavily armed man remained in the rear seat of each vehicle. They would be invisible behind the dark glass. If someone did approach the vehicles, I suspected they would be cut down in seconds.

Everyone went inside, except for the sentries in the vehicles and two more at each corner of the building. A few more people arrived who appeared to be government officials. All clearly knew Alejandro very well and I knew were either in his pocket or doing his bidding to keep their own secrets safe. I said I was going to go have a quick scan of the front and back just to feel extra safe. Alejandro laughed and told me knows this place, but if I must satisfy my need to keep him healthy and happy then I should do so.

I went out the front door, nodding to the two sentries and that was when I noticed a familiar couple at the restaurant next door. They were sitting out on the patio. It was Colin and Norie, clearly posing as a honeymooning couple of Americans. Dressed like your really touristy tourists they would have stood out anywhere else but here. Festival de la Cosecha seemed to be Bourbon Street, Rocky Horror Picture Show and any Western movie combined into one. There were all kinds of people, each dressed in their own unique getups.

I couldn't risk acknowledging them, so as I scanned the area, I just rubbed my right eye.

They were both sharp, they would know I now was aware I had backup. I was SO glad they had found me. It wasn't like we could shoot our way out against a dozen heavily armed men, most carrying Mac 10's with thirty shot clips, but at least they were there. I knew Colin would have wanted to see El Rey die but that was unlikely. It would be far too risky. I knew that me doing it myself was the safest way for us to escape.

We all sat in the restaurant eating and drinking as other guests continued to arrive. It was like a big birthday party. Mateo had explained protocols for various situations. If El Rey needed a private conversation, there was a table towards the rear in a secluded spot. He would take his guest back there and Mateo and I would stand in the narrow, dimly lit hallway, ensuring nobody could approach. That was also the hallway from which you accessed the washrooms.

While everyone was at the table, I told Mateo I had to use the facilities. I walked down the narrow hallway past the table and then turned right. There was a men's washroom on the left and the ladies on the right. Luckily, the men's room was on the outside wall. I was almost beside myself with excitement when I opened the door to the men's and found a small window. I was even happier when I confirmed that it was unlocked and led directly to the alley. It was small, but I knew I could squeeze through on an angle when the time came.

I was certain there would come a time when Alejandro would use the facilities and I knew that the only people close to that door would be Mateo and myself. While Mateo was wary of me, he would never expect me to take him out here in such a public place and surrounded by all his men.

I waited, sipping on my drink until finally Alejandro signalled Mateo, who indicated to me that he was going down the hall. Mateo went first, then El Rey then me. Mateo went ahead to ensure nobody was in either restroom and then Alejandro went inside. I knew this would be my best chance.

We both stood at the entrance to the short hallway, and I pretended my stomach was upset and told Mateo I would be right back. As I opened the ladies' room door, I reeled up my garotte from my packet. I was really hoping that Alejandro wasn't simply taking a leak as that would complicate things. I turned, made the loop, and quickly tightened it around Mateo's throat as I pulled him off his feet. I drug him back towards the ladies' room, using his own weight to accelerate his death as I tightened the garotte.

As he slumped, I could see the blood running down the front of his shirt while I drug him into the tiny room. I made sure he was dead, wiped the garotte on his shirt and locked the door behind me as I exited. Now it was time for the ultimate target.

I silently eased through the door, happy to see him inside the stall. He would exit the stall and then move to the sink, which would be on his left. There was a storage cabinet on the back wall, opposite the sink that I could crouch beside. I would be out of his view until it was too late. I got in position and waited, my garotte ready to go.

I heard the stall door open, and the water taps turned on. I could hear him soaping his hands and I came up behind him and locked in the garotte as I pulled him away from the sink. I strangled the life out of him while he kicked at the air, forced to listen to me talk about him killing my friend. He would know, in his last seconds on this earth, that he was being killed for a reason. Not for drugs or power but to avenge the death of my friend.

I whispered into his ear that he was as much bad as Patti was good, so I hoped he rotted in hell. I made sure the door was locked and then climbed out the window into the alley. As I was walking toward the corner one of our men was coming towards me. I had no idea if there was blood on me or if he could see if there was, but I could take no chances. I smiled at him as he got closer and at the last possible second shot out a vicious blow into the center of his throat. He collapsed, I got behind him and snapped his neck with a hard twist. I drug him behind the dumpster, calmed myself and moved slowly toward the front corner of the neighboring restaurant.

I was pleased to see Colin and Norie seated in the same spot, right against the outer rail and the sidewalk. I just nodded my head and Norie came around to the side of the building, directing me to their vehicle. It was a customized half ton truck with its most customized feature being a compartment hidden in the bed.

She motioned me into the back and hit a button. A section of the truck bed popped open. There was what appeared to be a 24-inch wide by 18- or 20-inch-deep compartment that ran the full length of the bed. It was nicely padded and even had a small light in it in case whomever was in there might be claustrophobic. I quickly climbed in, laid down and the lid was closed. Even though it was the tiniest of places, and not completely comfortable, I felt safe. My task was completed, and it appeared I had at least a fifty-fifty chance of getting away.

Soon I heard both doors close and we were driving off. It felt like about fifteen minutes later when the truck stopped, and I heard the engine shut off. I had a Tomcat in each hand as the cover opened. I heard Colin's voice saying it was just them, nobody else was around.

The truck was parked inside a garage, and I got out slowly, guns still in hand. When it was clear it really was just us, I climbed completely out, slipped the Berettas back into my jacket and hugged them both. I think the three of us stood there in a group hug for five minutes.

I recalled President Nieto's word and smiled at Colin, "Mission accomplished, he is gone." I looked at him and said I know you would have preferred captured and maybe you take him out, but I had no choice. This was the safest and best way to get it done.

We all went inside, and Colin poured us some wine. He smiled and asked me to tell him all about it. Did he fight? How did I do it? Was it slow? What look did he have on his face when I told him I was avenging Patti's death? Tell me how he sounded as you killed him? We shared two bottles of wine and agreed that it had been an awfully long day and that we can talk in the morning.

I slept more soundly than I had in many months. It was almost over.

Chapter 30 Six – The Aftermath

When I awoke in the morning Colin and Norie were already up and enjoying their coffee. Colin said this place had been in his family for years, so it was perfectly safe. It was in Patti's maiden name so there was no connection to him. They said they had gotten some decent intel from various sources, but it was sheer luck that they found me during the harvest festival. They had already been to four other restaurants when they settled into the one next door to Pitahaya Costes.

I imagine Los Mochis was going wild by now and that they were actively looking for me. We decided they most likely would have already contacted Arturo as that was where I came from. I explained they had something on me, and we would need to take them out. We all agreed that would have to happen rather than later.

I had no stamp on my passport entering Mexico, so I did not want to attempt to cross back legally. It would certainly be far too dangerous to go back to the boat but that was when I came up with the idea.

The three of us could go to the powerboat. We could take the boat, after disposing of whomever was there, and then contact Arturo. We would tell him that no matter what he had heard that I had El Rey with me.

There had been an attempt on his life by another cartel. Mateo was dead, but I had saved El Rey and driven us to the dock.

We agreed it was a solid plan and left soon after to go to the dock.

I was shocked when there was nobody at the small dock where the speedboat was stored along with the converted fishing boat, we used to move the girls. We watched the boats and the area for a couple of hours and saw nothing. We drove up, parked the truck, and boarded the Mystic boat. Fifty feet long and loaded with power. Colin worked on the ignition and controls for a bit and suddenly more than 4,000 HP of turbine engines roared to life.

He looked at the fuel gauges and said both tanks were full, glad these guys were always prepared to run. We headed South down the Gulf of California at a comfortable speed so as not to attract any interest. Getting caught in a stolen boat, in Mexican waters, with a couple of RPGs in the hold, would not do us any good. Badges didn't help down here either.

As we rounded Cabo and started to head North, I put in a call to Arturo. I sounded frantic as I described what had happened and told him he should get in a boat and meet us about halfway down the outside of the peninsula. He wanted to speak to El Rey, but I told him the boss had been hurt and he should bring the doctor on the boat too.

He said they would load up and meet us halfway, he expected about two hours with us moving towards each other. I had by now figured out that the massive, high-powered speedboat I had seen at Arturo's marina was the sister to this one. Knowing you could outrun anything on the sea was a nice feeling when you were a drug runner or other criminal. Now, I had to hope and pray that Arturo's protocols had all been followed.

Not only would Arturo be on the boat but so would Javier and a couple of other trusted people. It no longer mattered if he believed my story or someone else refuted it after the fact. They were on the boat hoping to either retrieve El Rey, and further ingratiate himself to his boss, or exact revenge on his killer, me! Either way, they would be the ones on the losing end of this exchange and Arturo would most certainly be on that boat.

As we approached an hour and a half since our call both Norie and I focused high powered binoculars out the bow towards the North. Thankfully, there were not a huge number of boats on the water. I caught a glimpse of what might be Arturo's boat about five miles away. I told Norie to keep an eye on them and let me know when she could make out faces. There was another telescope type unit mounted on a special pedestal next to the throttleman's seat.

As we motored steadily forward, we also discussed what would happen after. We would drive the boat as close to shore as practical, calculating we would be somewhere near El Rosario at the bottom of Baja California. Norie and I would hop out while Colin tied off the rudder to stay straight and then set the engines at a slow and comfortable twenty knot clip. From there we would make our way North, planning as we went. Although the FBI was supposed to focus on domestic issues there were a couple of safe houses in that area, complete with vehicles.

I looked through the telescope and was pleased to see both Javier and Arturo on the boat. We scanned the waters around us and there were no other craft in site. I was thankful there were so many fair-weather sailors.

Colin had two RPG launchers loaded and ready to go. They would have absolutely no idea what hit them. I would aim closest to Arturo and Javier and Colin would aim for the fuel tanks. There would be absolutely nothing left of the craft after that. It would sink quickly after the explosion, leaving little evidence. When it was discovered whose boat it was, the authorities would surely think they were just more casualties in a drug war. They would spend a minimal amount of time on the case and would likely thank us for doing what we did if they knew what we did.

Norie had moved to the pilot's seat and Colin and I were seated next to each other. He slowed the throttle down to around ten knots and we waited for smooth water. We assumed they would have binoculars on us too, so we knew we would have to aim and fire quickly.

We crept closer and closer and when they were less than two hundred feet away, we both steadied the launchers on our shoulders and hit the fire buttons simultaneously. We watched as the two projectiles shot out of the tubes, spinning swirling tails of fire as they moved toward the boat. At 920 feet per second, they had less than one quarter of a second to realize what was happening. By the time it registered in their minds, their boat would already be exploding into a massive fireball.

We watched as both rockets hit at the same time. They were called anti-tank weapons because of their destructive power, and that was when they pierced the thick armor of a tank. The fibreglass and Kevlar hull of that boat was certainly no match as it was obliterated. Where once had stood a fifty-foot behemoth of a speedboat, with six or eight men on it, now sat a growing oil slick and gasoline fire. There were bits and pieces everywhere.

We turned toward the shoreline and opened up the massive engines, propelling the boat forward like a rocket ship. We were driven back into our seats, unable to lift our heads off the headrests as we all held on for dear life. You could feel the water pounding under our feet as the twin hulls pierced the waves like knives. The shore came up on us far quicker than any of us expected so Norie eased off on the throttles while Colin kept control of the steering.

We were already close enough to get out, so Norie jumped out and started swimming while Colin and I readied the boat. We eased it around toward the most open water and tied off the steering to keep it straight. In a perfect world it would make it to the far-off island, crash into the shore and explode. If it did that would be great, but even if it didn't that would not change our plans. Once the steering was all set, I told Colin to jump out and I would set the throttles.

I eased them back and jammed two pieces of rubber in the throttle tracks just to make sure they stayed locked. Once the boat was heading off and everything looked good, I jumped over the edge and swam quickly back to shore. Even without fins I got there in no time, joining Colin and Norie on the shore. The three of us just sat there staring out into the ocean.

It was hard to believe it was mostly over. Sure, I would have to worry about being recognized for a while, but I kept to my own tight circle of friends, so I wasn't too concerned.

We agreed it would be safer to move at night. Turns out Colin figured we were less than five miles from the first safe house, and it was on the coast.

We would just hang out and start our trek soon.

I have always liked a nice walk on the beach, but it was a little different doing it this way.

A five mile walk on the beach in what was hostile territory with us possibly being pursued by the law or a drug cartel or both would not have been my number one choice.

But then, I was alive, the bad guys were dead, and the three of us had a chance to get away with it all. We just had to get out of Mexico.

Chapter 30 Seven – Getting Out Of Mexico

I was glad we didn't have to travel too far before coming to the safe house. We watched for about an hour to ensure there were no people anywhere around it and then headed straight to the garage. Inside were four dune buggy style side by sides. There was all kind of gear for men and women, including helmets and boots. These would be the ideal cover to get us up to the border. In this part of the beach there were dune buggies, quads, and side by sides all over the place. We would simply be three more tourists tearing it up.

There were clean passports that carried names and all the other information except photographs. There was a specialized camera along with a printer there so all we had to do was take the photos, insert them onto the passports and driver's licenses and then seal them. There were even Global Traveller passes that we personalized as well.

We all got into our gear, gabbed a couple of coolers full of snacks and water, donned our helmets and got ready to leave. From there it would be relatively easy to make our way North and then into Tijuana. We would board a commercial bus there to get back into the states, just three more weekend partiers returning home. It would be a simple story, and truthful because there was little doubt that we would be cutting loose a bit tonight.

We got everything set up and ready to go and we fired up the vehicles and took off up the beach. We bounced around the dunes as we made our way North, having a great time with little on our minds for the moment.

The sun was shining, the air was dry and the helmets and balaclavas, while warm, kept the sand out of our eyes. These machines had some power too. One had to be careful going up the dunes because if you gunned it too close to the top it was quite easy to flip. Although not a big deal as the roll cages were designed to right the vehicle if it did flip. Plus, three people could flip one back over onto its wheels if that was required.

We saw quite a few other people hooting and hollering as they shot huge plumes of sand into the air with their giant, finned tires. It was great to see so many others as that would make it even less likely we might be noticed.

After what seemed like hours of fun, we were rolling up close to Tijuana. We found a nicer looking hotel, at least for the area, and hopped off the vehicles. We parked them around back out of sight, grabbed our keys, and went to the desk.

We got a couple of rooms, paid cash, and picked up the bus schedule. We would likely leave the next night. We didn't see a rush as it was unlikely anyone would come after us. The federales had no idea who we were or what we had done. The drug cartels would immediately be scrambling for positions and even those in the Mochismo cartel would be focused on their own succession. After all, it didn't get much better than this, someone had killed their boss for them. Now it was only a matter of who would take over.

They would be in disarray for a brief time as things settled out, and usurpers to the crown were killed in battles. Soon a new leader would take hold of the organization. None of that mattered to us. We accomplished what we had wanted to accomplish. The person most responsible for killing Patti was dead. The top people who worked for him were dead. On top of it they had lost almost a million dollars worth of boats along with a whole bunch of cash. The Wounded Warriors Project would be receiving a great many contributions of cash over the coming years.

We all really liked the fact that cash was going to be put to good use. It was about time that drug money helped the world. After dropping helmets and keys and stuff in the rooms we went to try and find some clothing. Now we really fit in with the locals and tourists. It was time to find a place to party.

We would have preferred an excellent restaurant but didn't want to draw attention to ourselves. We decided on Republica Malta, more a mixology and beer spot than a restaurant. We thought it made the most sense, there were many local beers, and all were quite tasty. We got ourselves a good table, ordered the first round and some food and that got things started. We all danced a bit, drank a lot, and had a fun time. I was happy there were no issues or problems with drunks. It was a good thing to have a night out and not have some sort of problem crop up.

I have no idea what time we got back to our rooms and crashed but it was certainly early AM. The sun didn't even wake up Norie and I in our room. We heard a knocking at the door, and I sprang up, ready to take out whomever had come to get us. Thankfully, it was only Colin. I let him in as Norie remained sleepily lounging in her bed.

I got the sense she didn't have the same party genes that Colin and I did. She seemed just a little worse for the wear. Norie got out of bed to go take a shower, seemingly completely at home having Colin see in her in nothing but her underwear. I watched Colin's face and it seemed like he had seen this before.

He grinned at me sheepishly and said, "it's been going on for about two months now. It just happened." I forced out a smile and said I was happy for them, but I wasn't completely certain that I was. It's not like I had dibs on Colin or anything, I just got the assumption we might be headed toward something. I suppose I would have to be supportive and just go about my life.

Norie came out of the bathroom dressed and ready to go. I quickly got ready myself and we went to get bus tickets before we ate breakfast. We got our tickets for the 11:00 AM bus and then went to eat.

The 11:00 bus was always much less crowded as the hordes of Mexicans who worked around San Diego were already gone by that point. Soon we were rumbling northward on a rickety old bus and in no time stopping at the border.

The US Customs guys used to just walk inside the bus. You held up your passport and anyone they wanted to speak with was left behind to catch the next bus IF they were even allowed to enter. With all the border issues now around illegals they were more concerned about that than finding drugs. We all disembarked and lined up. We presented our Global Entry Trusted Traveller cards along with our passports. The guy looked at us, asked if we had a good time in TJ and that was it, we were through.

We got to the central train/bus station in old San Diego and grabbed an Amtrak North. We were going to head straight to Colin's house and then get ourselves arranged from there. I sure hoped I wasn't about to see that Norie had moved in. I sat by the window and looked out at the ocean as we rumbled northward on the seaside track.

We got a taxi from the Amtrak station to Colin's and soon we were all sitting on the deck, staring out at the ocean. I couldn't help but recall how those RPGs had completely obliterated that boat, along with Javier, Arturo and whomever else was on board. Those things had a ridiculous amount of destructive power.

It was early, but Colin got a bottle of wine and we all toasted to our success. We agreed that was that and we would not talk about it at all going forward. We were closing that chapter in our lives and now we could all get on with living again.

As if on cue, Colin's phone rang, and it was Jonathan asking if he was up for a party this weekend. Colin handed the phone to Norie and then she handed it to me. We all confirmed we would love to attend. I was excited about getting back to normal. At least, what I had now come to accept as normal. I was already looking forward to getting back to my own gym, sparring with my usual partner and even lunches with Angela and Kathy.

I couldn't wait to sleep in my own bed either. Come and go as I please, and SURF!

I had left a bike at Colin's so once we were done wine and snacks, I took off back to my house. It was almost strange walking back in there after so long. It was like everything was new again. It seemed everywhere I looked I was seeing something that felt new.

I went almost straight to my shower to relax and clean off whatever I could. That was a long time undercover for me and I needed to get back to my own, real, routine as soon as possible.

For me, that was the best way to avoid the typical PTSD one might get from doing what I did. Of course, this was another story I could share with almost no one. At least this time I could talk to Norie and Colin about it.

As isolated as I had been when I was working for the government, I still needed to be able to share these things sometime.

Chapter 30 Eight – Party Time!

I had a relaxing few days at home and the party seemed to come up on me without warning. Suddenly, it was noon, and I got a call from Norie asking when I was going over to Kathy and Jonathon's? I had also forgotten it was one of those "start in the afternoon" deals. I immediately thought of surfing though and that really helped get me motivated.

I threw a few things into a bag, including a night shirt with my rash guard and favorite swimsuit. While working with Arturo and El Rey it seemed I was either in a suit, strapped with at least two weapons, or running gear. I don't recall being dressed any other way. Oh well, I was done with that now. It was time to get back to doing the things I really liked.

Norie swung by and picked me up and on the drive over she said that nothing really happened with her and Colin. She added that they were now over anyway and decided to just stay friends. Norie had a lot on her plate as a top ADA and Colin was basically working two jobs while we were hunting down El Rey. I think they were both there for each other when each needed something. It happens.

We rolled up to Kathy's and before we were even out of the car Kathy and Angela almost swarmed us first and right behind them Luke and Jonathon. They were anxious to know where we had been, what I had been doing, all the things I could not talk about. We had agreed that the story we would stick to was that I was doing some undercover work for Colin. It was nothing we could talk about of course. At least there was truth to the story, which made it cleaner. I WAS under cover, and I WAS working for Colin. That made it a little easier to lie to our friends. I was quite sure they would find what I did distasteful at best. After all the hugs, hellos, and welcome backs, we all went through the house to the patios.

Things were really hopping, and Jonathon went directly back to his treasured BBQ to continue cooking up appetizers for everyone. We all had some light snacks, maybe one drink each and suddenly there was eight or nine of us on boards out pounding the waves. It was another perfect surf day, and I was loving every second of every wave. It was so good to be out riding with my friends again. Nobody to kill, nobody to blow up and no idiots to worry about.

It was just me, my friends, and the glorious waves of Southern California. As we were waiting for a wave Norie leaned over to me and said she might have some work for me. Would I be interested? I said I might be, and we can talk about it next week.

Right now, all I wanted to do was surf with all my friends.
Other books by C.C.Chamberlane
ABBADON

C.C.Chamberlane's first book detailing Meg's re-entry to "normal" life after leaving the Special Forces. She was a formidable woman who had always had a calling, but one unhealthy relationship would completely reorient per priorities.

The First Female Navy SEAL – Megan Hernandez

Learn about Megan's upbringing and the challenges she faced trying to secure her spot in one of the last bastions of macho maleness. No female had ever come close to become a SEAL but then the Navy had never before seen anyone like Meg Hernandez.

Saving Ukraine

Megan Hernandez and two of her former SEAL teammates save children, eliminate Somali pirates and then take out the madman leading Russia against the Ukraine.

Don't miss out!

Visit the website below and you can sign up to receive emails whenever C. C. Chamberlane publishes a new book. There's no charge and no obligation.

https://books2read.com/r/B-A-JWSR-PNUVB

BOOKS 2 READ

Connecting independent readers to independent writers.

Did you love *Samaela*? Then you should read *Abbadon*[1] by C. C. Chamberlane!

[2]

ABBADON is the first in an action adventure series detailing the exploits of Megan Hernandez. She is a very powerful and dangerous woman who has the government-trained skills to kill easily with many different weapons, especially her hands. She is fearless in executing her tasks and missions and will stop at nothing to get the job done.

---

1. https://books2read.com/u/bxQOk6

2. https://books2read.com/u/bxQOk6

Also by C. C. Chamberlane

Megan Hernandez
Samaela
The First Female Navy SEAL
Saving Ukraine

Standalone
Abbadon

About the Author

C.C.Chamberlane has been a novelist for a few years now. His first series of books include; ABBADON, SAMAELA, the First Female Navy SEAL and Saving Ukraine.

These stories focus on Megan Hernandez and her power and commitment to do good in the world.